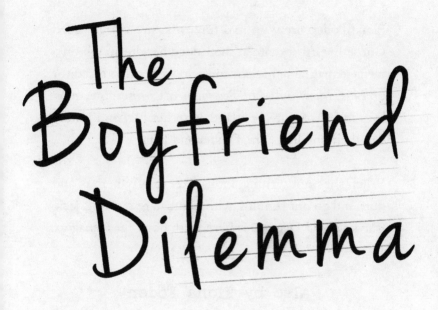

The Boyfriend Dilemma

D0784746

About the Author

Fiona Foden grew up in a tiny Yorkshire village called Goose Eye. At seventeen she landed her dream job on a teenage magazine in Scotland, and went on to be editor of *Bliss*, *More!* and *Just Seventeen* magazines. She now lives in Lanarkshire, Scotland, with her husband Jimmy and their children Sam, Dexter and Erin.

When she's not writing, Fiona likes to play her sax and flute and go out running with her mad rescue dog, Jack. *The Boyfriend Dilemma* is her fourth book for teenagers.

Also by Fiona Foden

Life, Death and Gold Leather Trousers
Cassie's Crush
A Kiss, a Dare and a Boat Called Promise

The Boyfriend Dilemma

Fiona Foden

SCHOLASTIC

First published in the UK in 2014 by Scholastic Children's Books
An imprint of Scholastic Ltd
Euston House, 24 Eversholt Street
London, NW1 1DB, UK
Registered office: Westfield Road, Southam, Warwickshire, CV47 0RA
SCHOLASTIC and associated logos are trademarks and/or
registered trademarks of Scholastic Inc.

Text copyright © Fiona Foden, 2014
The right of Fiona Foden to be identified as the author
of this work has been asserted by her.

ISBN 978 1407 14529 7

A CIP catalogue record for this book is available
from the British Library.

All rights reserved.
This book is sold subject to the condition that it shall not, by way of
trade or otherwise, be lent, hired out or otherwise circulated in any
form of binding or cover other than that in which it is published.
No part of this publication may be reproduced, stored in a retrieval
system, or transmitted in any form or by any means (electronic,
mechanical, photocopying, recording or otherwise)
without the prior written permission of
Scholastic Limited.

Printed and bound by CPI Group (UK) Ltd, Croydon, CR0 4YY
Papers used by Scholastic Children's Books are made
from wood grown in sustainable forests.

1 3 5 7 9 10 8 6 4 2

This is a work of fiction. Names, characters, places,
incidents and dialogues are products of the author's imagination
or are used fictitiously. Any resemblance to actual people, living
or dead, events or locales is entirely coincidental.

www.scholastic.co.uk

For Esme and Orla with love.

Chapter one

Zoe

Ever had *one of those days*? I have no idea that it's going to turn out to be one of them when I wake up. In fact, everything feels pretty perfect. The sky is a brilliant blue and, although it's 8.15 on a Monday morning, there's no Monday feeling at all. It's the Easter holidays and I have a whole day with my best friend Layla ahead. What could be better than that?

But first, duty calls. Mum, who's a plastic surgeon, has been called into work for an emergency, so I have to take my little brother Matty to holiday club. I pull on jeans and a plain white T-shirt and call for Matty to get up. When no reply comes, I yell, "MATTY! Mum had to go to work so I'm taking you to holiday club. C'mon!" Still nothing. I march towards his room, pulling my hair back into a ponytail with the band from my wrist. Holiday club starts at nine so there's no time for messing about.

No Matty in his room. I know he's already up, though, as his bed's been made with the duvet smoothed over (Mum is *horribly* strict about things like that). He must be hiding somewhere; at nine years old, he still finds it hilarious to bounce out from his hiding place, roaring like a monster. *Will he ever grow out of this?* I actually think his main ambition is to give me a heart attack. Then he'd get my room, which he reckons is "better" because the big window opens out onto a balcony. "Matty!" I shout. "Come on – we've got to *go*."

Still silence. I check the upstairs bathroom and peer into Mum's bedroom, even though it's unlikely he's in there – she keeps it so perfect you feel like you're messing it up just by breathing. If that makes her sound scary, she's not at all – just immensely organized and crazily busy being the best paediatric plastic surgeon in Britain. She treats kids who've had horrible things happen to their faces or bits of their bodies, and she's been in the newspaper and even on TV.

I could kill Matty for messing me about. It's now half eight and I still have his packed lunch to make. It's horribly tempting to make him something like, I don't know, an anchovy sandwich – just to get my own back. "Matty!" I keep shouting, starting to actually worry now. Has something happened? He might be the most annoying nine year old ever to have walked the earth, but he's still my brother and he's always having freak accidents. When he fell off his bike and broke his arm, he had a long, thin piece of metal inserted into it, like a tent peg. My throat starts to tighten as I check the garden. Nothing. I march back into his room, my gaze skimming his bed, his shelf with the empty fish tank still sitting on it (Jaws died last year) and his boxes of toys on the floor.

That's when I spot it: a small, pale arm poking out from behind his wardrobe. It's flopped out on the carpet, lifeless and covered in blood. My mouth falls open but no sound comes out. Some of the blood is bright red and looks wet, while other parts are darker, nearly black, where it's dried into scabs. "Matty," I croak, forcing myself to step forward. "Oh my God, what happened. . . ?" My heart seems to stop as I reach the wardrobe and peep behind it.

And . . . there's *nothing there*. No dead brother – not even an injured one lying in a pool of blood. It's just a plastic arm, from a shop mannequin by the look of it, splattered in paint. "April fool!" Matty bellows behind me. I spin around to see him laughing his face off in his baggy Darth Vader underpants.

"You're *sick*, you know that?" I grab the arm and wave it at him like a truncheon, managing to cover myself in paint.

"You thought I was dead!" he guffaws.

I glare at him. "Wait till I tell Mum. Where did you get this anyway?"

Matty smirks. "Found it."

"Oh, right, 'cause there are always plastic body parts lying about in the street. . ."

"It was in a skip," he adds, "outside that old ladies' dress shop."

See how warped he is? He must've figured that it'd be ideal for tormenting me. As if I need this, at the start of the Easter holidays, after the terrible time I've had at school lately. Seriously – the past couple of weeks have been hell, ever since Mum appeared on TV. She was on this science programme, being interviewed about the amazing operations she's been doing, using fake skin that's grown in a laboratory. Sure, I think she's amazingly clever – but d'you know what happens when your mum's on TV? You're no longer an ordinary girl in a smallish town where nothing much ever happens. All of a sudden, you're "spoiled", a "snob" and "think you're something special *because of your famous mum*". As if she's a pop star or an actress who spends all her time going to celebrity parties and movie premières.

I wanted to shout, "I'm still *me* – the same person I was yesterday – and my mum's only a doctor. It's no big deal. . ." But I couldn't – not when Carla Jamieson had started the whole thing. Carla calls herself CJ because she thinks it sounds hard, and although I hate to admit it, she actually is. She hacks at her own hair with kitchen scissors and roams around with her big sister Toni and their mates, looking for people to torment.

Toni is even scarier than CJ. She has an electronic

tag on her ankle so the police know where she is all the time. It's like radar, but instead of being for boats or planes, it's for tracking a seventeen-year-old girl who's been in trouble for starting fights and setting fire to bins. So, the Jamiesons – let's just say it's a good idea to stay out of their way. Anyway, I wasn't about to report CJ for calling me a snob.

"Just rise above it, darling," Mum advised, so that's what I've been doing: imagining myself as a cloud, about to gush freezing rain all over CJ's head. I've also considered giving myself an "initials" name of my own – but that would be ZH, for Zoe Harper. As well as being pretty awkward to say, it's not exactly intimidating. Anyway, I've been counting the days until the Easter break. Even though I'm bound to run into CJ at some point, at least I won't have to sit in classes with her every day and have her hissing, "*Your* face looks like it was made in a laboratory, snob."

In the kitchen, Matty is still sniggering over his genius prank. It's so fantastically amusing that he's even forgotten to moan about our gravelly muesli like he usually does. So at least I'm spared that. But I still want to ping him into holiday club as quickly as possible and head over to Layla's, where life is normal. No twisted pranks, no mum on telly talking about cow skin – Layla has no idea how lucky she is.

By the time we arrive at the sports centre, all the kids have been dropped off. There's a rowdy game of softball going on in the main hall, so I grab my brother's hand and find a friendly-looking helper. "Sorry we're late," I say. "This is Matty Harper—"

"I got her with an April fool," he blares out, still delighted with himself. "I covered a fake arm in paint mixed with soil so it looked scabby. She thought I'd been murdered, haha!" *Go on, Matty. Tell her some more in case you haven't convinced everyone that our family's completely weird*. . . I force out a laugh to prove I can take a "joke".

"That was clever," the girl chuckles, searching for his name on her clipboard. "Matty Harper . . . ah, here you are." She turns to me. "How old are you?"

"Er, thirteen," I reply, realizing with a sickening feeling what's coming next.

"Sorry, you have to be over sixteen to sign him in."

"Please," I say quickly, dreading the thought of looking after Matty for eight life-sapping hours. "Mum was meant to bring him but she was called into hospital. She's a doctor—"

"A famous plastic surgeon," Matty says proudly.

The girl tilts her head. " Was she on that programme about cow skin?"

"Yes, that was her," I murmur, hoping no one else has overheard.

The girl's eyes widen. "It was amazing. I mean, cow skin! It's kinda. . ." She shudders. "It's a bit *eugh*, but then, if it helps children who've been burned or whatever. . ."

"Cow skin?" sniggers another helper, marching

towards us, her shiny plaits bouncing above her shoulders. "You mean like beef? Or burgers?" My face is blazing now. *No*, I want to shout. *Mum doesn't fix kids' faces with burgers. She uses stuff that looks exactly like human skin, but is grown in Petri dishes from cow proteins. . .* Oh, never mind. I don't fully understand it myself, being a schoolgirl and not a world-class surgeon who spent about a hundred years at university. . .

"Let her sign him in, Kate," the plaits girl says, grabbing the clipboard and pen and handing them to me. "No one'll know." She smiles down at my brother who's busily picking wax from his ear. "Got your packed lunch, love"

He looks up at me. "Where's my packed lunch?"

"Oh, I . . . forgot."

"But I'm here all day!" he gasps. "I'll *starve*." He clutches at his stomach as if he's about to collapse.

"I'll buy you something," I snap, figuring that I'd rather spend pretty much all of the five-pound note in my pocket than have to go home and make him something when I could be at Layla's. The sandwiches in the newsagent's over the road look pretty sad, but I buy one anyway, plus a bottle of apple juice and some crisps.

Matty glares at his sandwich as if I'd scraped it up off the pavement. "You know I hate tuna," he yells as I race for the door.

Chapter two

Layla

Our house is full. Fuller than normal, I mean – which is saying something, because there's a lot of us jammed into a pretty small place. While Mum makes breakfast downstairs (she does the best, crispiest bacon in the world and the smell is drifting up the stairs), a whole gang of boys are chatting and laughing in my big brother's room. Kyle had a pile of friends to stay over last night. The boys don't call them sleepovers. Sure, they stuff their faces with popcorn and crisps, watch movies and chat late into the night. Which is exactly the same as a sleepover, right? Except the films Zoe and I watch tend not to be about some creepy guy lurking about in the basement, waiting to chop a bunch of teenagers into little bits.

Mum doesn't mind people staying over. Dad doesn't really notice because he works long hours as a taxi driver – even when he is at home, he's usually asleep on the sofa with his mouth wide open. And Gran, who lives with us too because she gets confused sometimes, likes lots of people around. Until last year she was living in her tiny cottage in the hills, but Mum and Dad were worried about her all the way out there, and Mum gave up her job to look after her. After she moved in with us, Gran told me, with a big, wide smile, "It's impossible to feel lonely in this house."

Well, that's true. Sometimes, though, I think maybe a smidge of loneliness might be OK. And occasionally, when my little sister Amber's jewellery-making stuff is covering every inch of our shared room, I picture myself in Zoe's amazing bedroom – actually *being* Zoe, with her queen-sized bed and her balcony. She's even got a table and two chairs out there where she can sit and think – and no one bothers her, ever. We just have a tiny back yard with the wheelie bins and a plastic chair with a cracked seat we put out for Gran to sit on when she has her "morning cigarette". Whenever Gran says it – "*my morning cigarette*" – she puts on a posh voice as if there's something almost royal about it. Like the queen might have her *morning cigarette* before receiving guests in the drawing room. . .

Unusually, I *am* alone now. Amber is downstairs with Mum, and I'm lying fully dressed on my bottom bunk, listening in on the conversation next door. I don't feel guilty, OK? For one thing the walls are paper thin – it's impossible *not* to overhear things. Also, it's payback. A few months ago Kyle installed a "spying device" (just a tiny microphone really) in my room when Zoe and I were singing, and recorded us. We used to sing all the time. Not any more – not since he played it to his friends and they all starting mimicking us for weeks, like it was the funniest thing in the world. Can you believe someone would do that at his age? Isn't he supposed to be *mature*?

Naturally, I recognize most of the voices coming from his room. Apart from my brother with his big, loud laugh, there's also Danny, Harris and Jude, who've been friends of his since for ever (we have lived here, in our little terraced house, all our lives). But there's a new voice too, one I don't recognize. I listen as hard as I can.

His accent is different, kind of posh and definitely not from around here. Not *royal* posh, but confident and clear as he tells the boys about the bands he's seen – and he's seen *everyone*. It's unbelievable. I've never even been to a proper gig. Who *is* he? I lie there still as a corpse, earwigging.

"So why did you move here?" Kyle asks.

"Dad's job," the new boy replies. "He works in the music industry and—"

"What, in this dump?" Danny exclaims. "There's nothing like that around here."

"He'll be working in Glasgow," New Boy explains, "where this big new recording studio's been set up. But Mum wanted us to live somewhere quieter, more peaceful. . ."

Jude's laugh rings through the wall. "More boring, you mean. Can't believe you left Brighton to come up here." Although he's Danny's little brother – in the same year as Zoe and me – Jude doesn't act young. He's funny and smart and, to be honest, he's by far the best musician out of all of them. The four of them are in a band together. Kyle plays drums, Jude sings and plays guitar, Danny's on bass and Harris – well, he sort of hangs about, pointing out how they *should* be doing things.

"I don't think it's boring," the boy remarks. "I kinda like it."

"Where's your house?" Danny asks. "Bet it's massive. . ."

"It's OK," the boy says, sounding embarrassed.

"C'mon," Harris teases him. "What's it like? Which street is it in?"

There's some mumbling and sniggering as the boys nag him to tell them exactly where he lives. "I'll show you sometime," he says. I feel sorry for him; he clearly doesn't want to show off and make a big deal of it.

Even so, I'm desperate to know more. Maybe he lives in some grand place that's even bigger than Zoe's. That's probably it. I try to picture the few big houses dotted around here – like Dean House, with its turrets and orchard and the angry owner who threatened to call the police when me and Zoe snuck in and stole apples.

"You coming to Mossbridge after the holidays?" Kyle

asks, meaning the school we all go to just down the road.

"Yeah."

"What was your old school like?" Danny wants to know.

"All right, y'know. Pretty relaxed."

"You're lucky," Jude sniggers. "Mossbridge isn't relaxed at all. . ."

"Was it one of those arty places where you only have to do lessons if you feel like it?" Kyle asks.

"Er, kind of," the boy replies. Someone's put music on now, so all I can catch are occasional phrases like "boarding school" and "trip to China", which, to me, mean "*incredibly* posh". Our school trip last year was to France, and Mum and Dad couldn't afford for me and Kyle to go. Instead, they took us all (including Gran) on a day trip to the seaside, where Amber saw a poo floating in the sea.

I get up from my bed and tiptoe to the bathroom before this new person can see me. With the door locked, I brush my teeth as thoroughly as possible, even though I'll have to do it again after breakfast. I even floss, like Zoe does. For some reason, it seems vitally important to have gleaming teeth today.

Back in my room, I check my reflection in the mirror on the wardrobe door, hoping the clothes I threw on earlier don't look too mad. Paisley-patterned shirt, beaten-up denim shorts with flowery-patched pockets, thin red belt to hold them up (as they're a teeny bit too big), plus purple tights ... is it all a bit too much? I'm so used to picking out charity-shop clothes that I'm pretty sure I can throw an outfit together. Zoe reckons I have "natural style" – but then, she'd hardly say, "God, Layla – where did you get that shirt from? The clothing bank?" It's next to the bottle bank in the park. CJ spread a rumour that she'd seen me squeeze myself into the hole where people post their worn-out clothes, trying to get stuff out. "Her bum and legs were sticking out," she announced, making out I was that desperate for something to wear. I have no idea why CJ hates me and Zoe. She calls Zoe a "snob" and me a "tinker", so you can't win really.

You look fine, I tell myself firmly. Why am I feeling so self-conscious all of a sudden? Probably because, although charity shops are OK, occasionally I wish I could go to all the normal high-street shops like Zoe does and, you know, look normal. Much easier that way. I glance at my alarm clock and wish she'd hurry up.

"Layla!" Mum calls upstairs. "Kyle, boys ... there's a whole stack of waffles here. Hurry up before they go cold." Eek – I'm about to meet *the voice*. The rich-dad-in-music-business, school-trip-to-China new arrival. I try to flatten my dark springy curls and run my tongue over my shiny teeth. "Plenty for everyone," Mum adds cheerfully. I hurry downstairs to get myself settled all *casually* at the kitchen table before the boys arrive. By some miracle, Mum has managed to cram eight seats – including our wobbly piano stool – around the kitchen table.

Gran, who's nearly eighty and hates being left out, is already sitting there, stuffing her face with several slices of bacon squashed between a couple of waffles (she likes to eat everything in a sandwich). Amber helps herself to a clump of rashers from the towering plateful, giggling, "Whoops – they were all stuck together." From under the grill comes another batch, and from upstairs comes a gang of boys, five of them all laughing loudly and clattering towards us. I sit next to Gran, wondering why I'm feeling so edgy in my own house as they all pour in: Kyle, Danny, Harris, Jude and *him* – New Boy – wearing jeans and a pale blue T-shirt with a scratchy drawing of a polar bear on the front.

"Make room for Ben," Mum says as everyone grabs seats.

The stool next to me is empty. I look up at the boy and he smiles down at me. It's the biggest, sunniest smile I've ever seen. His eyes are so blue they're almost unreal, and his honey-ish hair is just the right kind of messy, all mussed around his face. Sensing my cheeks flushing hot, I quickly focus on my plate.

"You can sit next to Layla," Mum prompts him with a smile, as if she's a little bit impressed by this newcomer too. "Oh, I am being rude," she adds. "I haven't introduced you to everyone, have I?"

"That's OK," Ben says brightly, perching on the stool beside me. My heart starts rattling along at about twice its normal speed.

"That's Amber," Mum continues. "She's eight. And this is Frances — we don't talk about your age, do we, Mum?"

Gran sniggers and takes a noisy slurp of her tea. "Don't mind me with my shoes off," she says. "My bunions are hurting—"

"Oh dear," Ben says with a sympathetic smile.

"You do have slippers," Mum reminds her gently as Amber's shoulders shake with silent laughter. Great. First impression Ben has of our family, and Gran introduces her poorly feet. "And this is Layla," Mum adds. "She's the one in the middle. . ."

"Hi," I murmur, wishing she didn't describe me like that whenever we meet someone new.

"Hi, Layla," Ben says. I smile, trying to look relaxed, and take a sip of tea from the "Layla" mug Zoe brought me back from holiday last year. I reach for a waffle but it tastes like cardboard, even with Nutella smeared on. I take another sip of tea and pray that Gran keeps her feet on the floor and doesn't try to *show* everyone her bunions. When someone raps on the front door (no one ever gets around to putting new batteries in the doorbell), I almost cry out in relief and leap up to answer it. At least a few seconds away from the table will give my face a chance to cool down.

"Hey," Zoe says, all smiles, her long blonde hair pulled back into a neat ponytail. Her T-shirt and jeans look brand new, and she smells great. Zoe has a choice of expensive perfumes, while I just use the cheapest body sprays Mum gets me from the supermarket.

"Come in," I say, wanting to tell her all about Ben but knowing we'll have to wait until later to discuss him.

"Hi, Zoe," Mum says. "Have you had breakfast, love?"

"No, it was a bit of a rush this morning. . ." She grins at me, as if to say, *Wait till I tell you*, then her expression changes as she spots the new person at our table.

"This is Ben, a friend of Kyle's," Mum explains, putting a big jug of orange juice on the table.

"Hi," Zoe says quickly. Mum fetches Gran's chair from the yard and squeezes it in between Kyle and Jude. Now that Zoe's here, I feel less outnumbered by boys. My only worries are:

1. Am I managing to eat nicely, like a thirteen year old should be perfectly capable of doing, or have I somehow smeared Nutella around my mouth?
2. Are the purple tights a bit much?
3. And the patterned shirt? I loved it when I found it in Oxfam but does it look like I stole it off Gran?
4. What I'm going to say as BEN IS TALKING DIRECTLY TO ME?!

"Er . . . sorry?" I blurt out, realizing I haven't heard a word. All I can think is, his eyes are as blue as that blue angelfish we had at primary school – the one that attacked all the other fish until there were no others left in the tank.

"Could you pass me the juice please?" Ben asks politely.

"*Suuuuurre,*" I drawl, which comes out sounding ridiculous – like I've turned American or something. Jude gives me a confused look and Zoe widens her eyes. I reach for the jug and clonk it down in front of him.

"Could I have the butter as well, please?"

Such manners! Maybe Kyle could learn a thing or two from him? "No problem," I say, detecting a glimmer of amusement in his eyes.

"Uh, you've got a bit of chocolate. . ." Ben says. Now all eyes are on me, and Amber is giggling with her hand clamped over her mouth.

"Have I?" I prod at my face. "Where?"

"There," he says, pointing to the corner of my mouth. I rub at it with a finger.

"No, *there*." Ben reaches over and touches my cheek. It's like a mini electric shock zapping through my body. I rub again, catching Zoe staring at me across the table. The two of us are so close we can normally communicate almost telepathically. But this time I can't pick up her message at all.

"Has it gone now?" I ask, wondering if he can hear the *thump-thump* of my heart.

Ben frowns and touches my face again, making me almost tumble off my chair. I wipe my fingers around my mouth, cheeks and chin but judging by the smirk on Ben's face, I *still* haven't managed to get the smear off. Now I'm rubbing my sleeve over my mouth, not caring if it gets chocolatey. Zoe is waggling her eyebrows as if she's trying to transmit something to me — but what? And now Ben is laughing, and the sniggers ripple around the table until Jude blurts out, "Layla — he's just messing about. There's nothing on your face. You're *fine*, all right? You can stop scrubbing. . ."

"Oh!" I force out a laugh.

"Sorry, Layla," Ben says, grinning as he reaches for a waffle. "Couldn't resist that. April fool."

Chapter three

Zoe

I would've been happy to hang out at Layla's because, let's face it, it was pretty interesting around there. I mean – that boy. Ben with the zingy blue eyes, cheeky smile and actual *cheekbones*, like a boy model's, features that added up to the most amazing face I've ever seen. Where did he come from – outer space?

"That was so embarrassing," Layla exclaims as we head out into the bright spring day.

"Don't worry, it was funny," I reply. "And I tried to signal that he was joking."

She splutters with laughter. "You *tried* to signal?"

"Yeah!"

"Why didn't you just tell me, instead of watching me trying to rub non-existent Nutella off my face?"

We're both giggling away but I'm not sure I know the answer. Of course I should have said something. I could hardly think straight, though – not with Ben sitting just a metre or so away. He's gorgeous – like no one I've ever met before – and he obviously liked Layla because she's so relaxed and friendly and always looks unique. Otherwise, why would he have pulled that Nutella trick? He was flirting with her – at least, I think he was.

To be honest, I don't really understand boys at all. I've only ever had one crush – and that was on Kyle, who I'd known for ever. It just hit me – *wham*! He wasn't just Layla's big brother any more, and the only boy I'd ever felt truly relaxed with. I was actually a little in love with him. Of course, I didn't tell Layla. She'd have died laughing because she thinks he's an idiot, and anyway, there's no way he'd ever have been interested in his little sister's best friend. So I *forced* myself to stop liking him. I gritted my teeth and repeated, *YOU CAN'T FANCY KYLE* about eight million times in my head. Sometimes I added, *KYLE BURNETT IS SO IMMATURE.* Why else would he find it so hilarious to hide his "surveillance device" (i.e. that crappy little microphone thing) in Layla's room? He recorded us *singing*, then played it to his friends – it was so humiliating. I love to sing, especially with Layla. We were in the Acorn Theatre junior choir all through primary school. But I'd never imagined Kyle listening to every note.

"So, what d'you know about Ben?" I ask as we wander towards the park.

"Not much," Layla replies. "I heard him telling the boys he's from Brighton and went to boarding school, and now he lives in some massive house near here. But he didn't say exactly where."

We turn into the alleyway that leads to the park. "Cute, isn't he?" I add with a grin.

"Er, you could say that." Layla laughs, her dark curly hair dancing around her cheeks.

"Is he going to our school?"

"Yep."

"God, imagine!" I shriek. "It'll be the most exciting thing to happen at Mossbridge since. . ."

". . . since for ever," Layla declares, and she's right. *Nothing* ever happens around here. A broken loo, or someone grazing their knee at netball – that counts for Really Big News at our school. As for someone new arriving? Well, I can't remember the last time that happened. At least, there's never been anyone like Ben. . .

"He's going to be so popular," I add, wondering why this makes me feel a tiny bit sad, until I remember that he's already Kyle's friend, which hopefully means he'll be around at their place all the time. Their house draws everyone in. It may be small and crowded, but their mum's so welcoming and there are always delicious things to eat – no sugar-free muesli there, which is the only "cereal" my mum ever buys.

We've reached the park now. A river snakes through it, sparkling in the April sunshine as if someone's gone mad with glitter.

"Hey," Layla says, nudging me. "Look at that!"

I peer into the distance where a huge, brightly painted lorry with "Dodgems" written on its side is pulling into the park. "What's it doing here?" I murmur.

"Looks like it's stopping," she says. "C'mon – let's see what's going on." As we pelt towards it a couple of men climb out. Being bolder than I am, Layla marches up to them. "Are you setting up here?" she asks.

"Looks like it, love," one of the men replies with a smirk. "Just the dodgems. We're trying it out, seeing if it's worth it. . ."

"We've never had anything like that here," Layla yelps. "When can we have a go?"

The man chuckles. "Give us a chance, will you? It'll be a few hours yet, about two-ish. . ."

Layla turns to me. "Shall we wait?"

"Of course," I say, grinning. "We've got all day, haven't we?"

"Remember to tell all your friends," the man calls out as we head back to the river. "The more, the merrier. . ."

Layla and I stop and look at each other. I can tell by her face that we've had exactly the same idea. "Maybe," she suggests with a mischievous smile, "I could ask Kyle if he wants to come. . ."

"Maybe," I say, pretending to act all casual.

"And *maybe* . . ." she adds, giggling now.

". . . he might bring Ben?" My heart quickens at the thought. "Worth a try, I guess."

She pulls out her phone from her shorts pocket and

texts her brother, showing me the message: *Dodgems in park open at 2. Wanna come?*

In a blink, Kyle replies: *Yeah.*

Layla and I glance at each other as the five boys head towards us. I'd hoped the dodgems would be all set up by the time they arrived, but nothing's happening yet.

"Is this it?" Danny asks, hands shoved in his pockets.

"Er, yeah," I say, unable to meet Ben's eye. Maybe we shouldn't have asked them. Coming from Brighton, he's probably been to amazing theme parks. I realize now how pathetic this looks.

"It's better than nothing, isn't it?" Jude offers. "Stop complaining, Danny."

"Looks great," Ben adds, and I can't tell if he's being sarcastic or not.

"C'mon," Kyle says. "Let's see what's happening." As we all head over, Ben falls into step with me.

"So you're Zoe?" he says.

I smile stiffly. "Yeah." It's the first word I've managed to say to him. God, what's wrong with me? The other boys are all chattering away, but I can't think of a single thing to say.

"Kyle was moaning how boring it is around here," he adds. "But having a ride show up like this – that's not bad."

I nod mutely, wishing my brain would work properly. I'm good at loads of things, like science and long-distance running, but what use are those when a gorgeous boy is walking beside me in the sunshine?

"Are you having a go, Zoe?" Kyle asks, as one of the men turns on the music and lights.

"Sure," I reply. Then I remember – I had to buy Matty's lunch. "Oh – I don't have enough money," I mutter, flushing pink.

"Neither do I," Layla wails. "I forgot my purse. . ."

Kyle sighs and rolls his eyes. "S'pose I've got enough for a couple of goes. . ."

"Thanks," she says, and my spirits lift as we scramble into a car. Ben and Kyle grab another, while Jude and Harris hop into a third. Danny climbs into a car by himself and we all set off, driving cautiously at first, then speeding up and crashing into each other as the music blares out.

"Look out!" Layla screams as Ben, who's driving, slams into our car head-on. She presses her foot down and grips the steering wheel, and when I glance back, he's grinning straight at me as his car chases ours around the arena. I feel as if I can hardly breathe. Word must have flown around town about the dodgems because people have started to arrive. Jude's car whacks into ours again and again, and we're all screaming with laughter until it's time to climb out.

"That was great," I exclaim, not caring that my ponytail band has fallen out and my hair's all over the place. "Shall we go on again?"

"Yeah," Jude yells and we all pile back in. Our screams

of laughter are attracting a crowd and the man doesn't mind us having a few extra goes for free.

"That was brilliant," Kyle announces as we all come out and flop down beside the river. I glance over at Ben, aware of excitement fizzling inside me. He's changed everything, in just one day. The dodgems would have been fun without him, but somehow, he's made the day sparkle.

"So how did you meet Kyle?" I blurt out, determined to at least *say* something.

Ben arranges himself cross-legged beside Layla and me. "I went to that drop-in music session last Friday," he replies. At the Acorn, he means – our tiny local theatre where pretty much everything happens here: scouts, junior choir, Matty and Amber's Young Adventurers club (where they learn all kinds of survival skills, in case they happen to find themselves stranded with nothing but hedgehog to eat). "You're so lucky," he adds, "having a place like that."

"It's shutting down, though," I explain. "The roof was badly damaged in a storm just after Christmas, and they haven't been able to raise enough money to fix it."

"What'll happen to it?"

I shrug. "There's talk of it being turned into flats, if someone's willing to buy it in the state it's in. . ."

"You might have noticed the leaks and drips," Kyle adds with a smile.

Ben nods. "It'll be a real shame if it closes, though."

"There's a vintage market tomorrow to raise money,"

Layla adds. "But I doubt if that'll be enough."

I turn to Ben. "So what d'you play?"

"Guitar, and I sing a bit—"

Kyle bursts out laughing. "A *bit*?" He grins at us. "He's brilliant. You should hear him—"

"He's, like, professional standard," Jude chips in.

"He even writes his own songs," Harris adds. As Ben starts protesting that he's not that good, and the others argue that he really is, I wonder how the boys feel about this. They've been playing together for a year or so. No gigs yet – they reckon they're not ready – but I know that's what they're aiming for. So how will Ben fit in?

I glance at Jude, knowing how proud he is that he's one of the best guitarists at our school. Yet he doesn't seem remotely put out that Ben has impressed everyone after just one session at the Acorn. Every now and then, I sneak another look at Ben – his eyes are *amazing*. I try to picture him in Mossbridge High's gloomy uniform of grey trousers, black blazer and white shirt, and know he'll be surrounded by girls – girls from his year, not mine and Layla's. And he'll be too caught up with all that to bother with us.

"Want to see the rope swing?" Jude asks him.

"Sure," Ben says, and they all spring up and make their way towards the woods, where a gnarly old rope, with a log "seat", has hung from the conker tree for years now.

I pull off my trainers and socks and dip my toes into the cool river. "What a day," I murmur to Layla.

A smile lights up her face. "Amazing. . ."

"Have you ever met anyone like that?" I'm so glad it's just the two of us now, with the chance to discuss him.

"Never. I was thinking how his eyes are the colour of that fish at primary school – the blue angelfish, remember?"

"The only one that survived *the illness*?" I add with a smile. That's what Miss Farmer told us – that all the others had died of a mysterious disease during the night – trying to protect us from the truth that they'd been gobbled up by the one we'd imaginatively named Bluey. It was only on our last day at primary that she admitted he'd wanted the whole tank to himself.

Squinting in the sunshine, Layla looks over to where Ben is flying through the air on the rope. "Fancy a go?" she asks.

"OK," I say, trying to ignore another wave of shyness building up inside me. My phone buzzes in my pocket as I jump up. Five missed calls? Eek! Who's been trying to reach me? "Hello?" I say, answering the call.

"Is that Zoe, Matty's sister?" asks the female voice.

"Yes?" *God, what's he done now?*

"Holiday club closed twenty minutes ago," she adds sharply.

"Did it? Oh, I didn't realize. . ."

The girl sighs loudly. "Well, he's sitting here waiting for someone to pick him up. Everyone else has gone home and he's *very* upset."

Chapter four

Layla

I feel bad not going to the sports centre with Zoe, but she races off, shouting, "Stay here – I need to go NOW!" And she's gone in a flash, before I can even think of what to do next.

All right, that's not completely true. I *could* have gone, and run all the way with her and offered moral support in case Matty's in a real state and the holiday club helpers are mad at her. But then, would I really be any use? Zoe's a much faster runner than me – I'd only have held her back.

Anyway, today has been one of those days you wish would never end, and I want to stretch it as long as possible. I watch as the boys have a final go on the swing, then all head towards me, chatting as if Ben is part of the gang already. "You should come to our rehearsals," Kyle is telling him. "We need someone like you." I *think* a flicker of worry crosses Jude's face. . .

"Only if it's OK with everyone," Ben says, pushing back toffee-coloured hair.

"Course it is," Harris announces.

"Sure," Jude says brightly. "We could even play some of your songs."

"Really?" Ben sounds pleased.

"Yeah, why not?" Kyle looks over at me. "You coming home, Layla? Think everyone's heading back to ours for dinner. . ."

"Er, OK," I say, thinking, *Where else would I go?* I'm already feeling a whole lot less awkward around Ben. I've recovered from the Nutella incident, and if this is a taste of how the Easter holidays will be, I reckon they're set to be the best ever. . .

"Eating us out of house and home again," Mum exclaims as we all pile in, although Kyle and I know she doesn't mean it. She loves a bustling houseful and always manages to feed whoever turns up. "Sit down, everyone," she adds. "You've been out for hours – you must be ravenous." I grab the seat between Danny and Jude (sitting next to Ben again would seem *too* obvious). Chicken casserole is ladled onto plates, and Gran splits open a roll and stuffs it full of mashed potato. I'm so used to her weird eating habits, I've almost stopped noticing them. Now, though, I wish she'd just eat normally.

"This is lovely," Ben enthuses, making Mum glow with pride.

"It's delicious," Gran announces, chomping her roll

noisily. To make it worse, everyone's now too busy eating to chat, and Gran's slurpy mouth noises seem to fill the kitchen. Is she usually this loud, and we just don't notice? I glance at Ben, who's acting like everything's normal. Bet *his* family don't eat like this. He's finished his plateful already, and Mum laughs. "Wow, you have a good appetite, Ben. It's nice to see someone enjoying their food around here." Which is a little unfair, as Kyle, Amber and I all have huge appetites too. When there's not much money to spare, you don't grow up being picky.

Ben smiles and places his knife and fork neatly on his plate (maybe he was taught to be ultra-polite at boarding school?). Kyle and Amber have slung down their cutlery noisily, like we usually do. Gran's still sloshing her potato roll around in her mouth. For the second time today, I sense a prickle of guilt. First, I didn't race over to holiday club with Zoe. And now I'm ashamed of my own gran. . .

I glance at her, remembering the times before she started to get confused. When she'd take me, Zoe and Amber on *girls' adventures*, as she called them. We'd head out into the hills with a picnic in her backpack. Sometimes we'd go to the abandoned quarry and sit at the top, peering down into the great hole in the earth, waiting for the fox to come out.

He has a den down there, Gran told us. *If we wait long enough, he'll come.* She said she'd seen him, but I was never quite sure if she was making it up, because we never did.

"Layla?" Mum's voice snaps me back to reality.

"Huh?"

"I think someone's trying to talk to you," she says with a teasing grin.

Ben is looking at me and, for some reason, the other boys are all giving each other amused glances. Just like at breakfast, my cheeks feel like they're on fire. "Just wondering if you want to come up and watch a movie with us?" he says.

"Er . . . in Kyle's room?" I ask, turning even redder.

"Did we say we were gonna watch a film?" Harris asks. "I don't remember hearing that."

Now my face feels as if it could burst into flames.

"Anyway, Layla doesn't like the movies we watch," Danny announces.

"She hates horror." He gives me a patronizing look as if I'm five years old.

"Actually," I say, wondering if every mealtime's going to be as traumatic as this, "I really don't. Me and Zoe are more into comedies."

"Yeah," Jude says with a warm smile. "I don't blame you."

Danny snorts. "He has nightmares, y'know."

"No, I don't," Jude laughs, shaking his head at his big brother. "I just find them too samey."

Mum turns from the worktop and smiles. "Good for

you, Jude. You know your own mind. No need to follow the crowd all the time. . ."

Amber jumps up from her seat. "I'll watch your horror film, Kyle. I'm not scared of *anything*."

"Yeah, sure," he chuckles, turning back to his friends. "Anyway, maybe we'll go out instead, huh? Kick a football around the park?"

There's murmured agreement, and everyone thanks Mum for dinner as they all surge towards to the front door. Jude, who's last to leave, glances back and gives me a *wasn't-that-weird?* kind of look.

I smile and shrug, as if to say, *Yeah, whatever*. Gran's been taking everything in, though. "That new boy likes you," she teases when they've gone.

"Oh, Gran! Ben's just Kyle's friend. . ." *Agh, I have to get out of this kitchen. Now.*

"Kyle's friends don't usually invite you to watch movies," Mum observes, raising one eyebrow.

"He's just being friendly," I say firmly, getting up to clear the table and wondering why Ben wanted me to join them anyway. He probably *was* just being friendly. He doesn't realize that, every time he looks at me, I feel like the only person here − like he really sees *me*, and not just Kyle's little sister. It's weird, though. I mean, the boys never invite me to join in with stuff.

"Well," Gran adds as Mum helps her up from her chair, "I think he's just the boy for you, Layla. It's about time you found a nice boyfriend. . ."

"For goodness' sake," Mum splutters. "She's thirteen."

"D'you *love* him, Layla?" Amber squeals.

"Bye!" I say, legging it to my room, where my thoughts can soar, without my entire family trying to butt in.

Chapter five

Zoe

One thing that's far worse than a parent being mad is when they're "just so *disappointed*". That's what happens when Mum comes home from work, her face as flat as a grey afternoon.

"I was the last one there," Matty announces, even though he's already told her on the phone. "I said I'd be OK walking home on my own, but they wouldn't let me. Said it was against the rules—"

"Poor love," Mum says, before turning to me. "So what happened, Zoe? How on earth could you forget?"

"I just lost track of time," I say, feeling my cheeks burning pink.

"But how?"

I bite my lip, wondering how best to handle her. "Er, I don't know . . . I was just with Layla in the park and they started setting up the dodgems—"

"Dodgems?" Matty exclaims, making an instant

recovery at the mention of something that sounds fun. "Can I go? How long's it gonna be there?"

"Never mind that," Mum says firmly, fixing me with tired, pale grey eyes. "Zoe, I really needed to be able to rely on you today."

"I know, Mum," I mutter at our cream living-room carpet.

"I'm *very* disappointed. . ."

What else can I say? I can't change what happened, and I've apologized about a hundred times already. So I just nod and look sorry and wait for this to be over.

"Poor Matty," she adds, stroking his short fair hair.

He arranges his face into a suitably gloomy expression. "I had a horrible lunch as well."

This is *too* much. . .

"Really?" Mum asks. "What did Zoe make for you?"

"Nothing!"

Here we go.

"You went all day with nothing to eat?" Mum gasps.

"Yeah," he cries, and I swear he sucks in his cheeks to look thinner.

"Mum, he *did* have lunch," I cut in. "I didn't have chance to make it so I bought it from the newsagent's."

"A tuna mayo sandwich," Matty declares, "that tasted of sick."

Mum frowns at me. "You know Matty doesn't like mayonnaise and, anyway, there are plenty of things here for a packed lunch. Did you sleep in or something?"

I pause, incredibly tempted to say, "No – I was up in plenty of time. I just spent over half an hour looking for him, and you know what he'd done? Pretended he'd been murdered and nearly made me die of shock!" But you know what? I don't tell her because I want to *shame* Matty. I want him to realize what a generous big sister he has, and what a horrible little worm he really is. "We just ran out of time," I say quietly.

Mum perches on the sofa arm and sighs, as if disappointed by *life* now. Matty turns on the TV, which lightens the mood a little, and I start wondering what Layla and Kyle and the others – OK, Ben in particular – are doing now. Layla's mum doesn't mind if she stays out a bit late, as long as she's home before dark. And Layla isn't called *disappointing*. . .

"Anyway," Mum says, getting up and mustering a tight smile, "I've said my piece, Zoe, and I'm going to confiscate your phone for the next few days. That should teach you to be a bit more careful."

"Hahaha!" Matty guffaws, no longer looking as if he's about to die of starvation, I notice.

"That's enough, Matty," Mum says firmly. "Zoe, your phone, please."

"But, Mum!" I protest. "It's the holidays, I *need* it. . ."

She shakes her head. "I'm sure you can manage to communicate in other ways." As she holds out her hand, I fish my mobile from my pocket and hand it over.

"Like how?" I ask.

She frowns at me. "Well, if you want to see Layla, you could just go round there, couldn't you?"

"Or use our house phone to ring her house phone," Matty suggests, like he's some kind of genius. I could happily whack him with that plastic arm.

Mum's expression softens, signalling that the telling-off is over. "Listen, you two. What happened today made it clear to me that this isn't working. . ."

"What's not working?" I ask.

"This whole arrangement. Oh, it's just about manageable in term-time. I know you try really hard, Zoe, taking your brother to school and looking after him when I'm at work. And I know we get by, and I can rely on you – most of the time. But today made me realize—"

"We're *fine*, Mum," I interrupt. "It was just a mistake. I'll never do it again. . ."

She inhales slowly. "I've been thinking about it for a while anyway. I'm not sure it's fair on you . . . what with my shifts, and being on call—"

"What about Polly and Maya?" I ask. They've been our babysitters for the past few years. Not that I need a babysitter any more, but since she and Dad split up, Mum's been super protective.

"They're both going travelling after their exams," she explains. "And then they're off to uni. They won't be around for much longer."

"You mean we'll have to go to Dad's," I say glumly.

"That's not a permanent solution. He's *far* too busy." Hmm, a hint of bitterness there. It's not that I don't want to spend time with Dad. It's his girlfriend Rosalind and her daughter Olivia that I'm not so keen on – or their horses, for that matter. I mean, I *like* horses, from a distance (of about half a mile). I'm just not terribly keen on standing in the rain, watching an eleven-year-old girl trot around the paddock for what feels like weeks, while Rosalind stands there clapping and shouting encouragement like, "Beautiful turn! Lovely canter, darling! Oh, isn't she doing *marvellously*?"

"I'm thinking of getting some help," Mum adds.

"Mum, I'm thirteen!" I cry. "I'm too old for a nanny—"

She laughs, smoothing back her hair that she keeps cropped short and neat – less hassle that way. "No, love, I mean an au pair."

I glance at Matty, who's swung around from the TV. "What's an *au pair*?" he asks.

"Someone who helps out with childcare and housework and lives in," Mum explains.

"Lives in *what*?" he demands.

Mum laughs again. "'Lives in' means living in the house where they work. . ."

"What, so they'd live here, all the time?" I'm trying to ignore the anxiety swirling around in my stomach. I don't want a stranger living in our house. It's been weird since Dad left, but we're doing OK, just the three of us.

She nods. "That's the idea, yes. We have the spare room, which is hardly ever used. And we desperately need an extra pair of hands. . ."

"No, we don't," I exclaim. "We're fine as we are!"

She squeezes my hand. "No, we're not. It's too hard on you, and it's too stressful for me, Zoe. I need to know someone's here all the time." She heads for the door, beckoning us to follow her. "Come on, I've got something to show you."

The *something* is an au pair website on her laptop. "I've already put in our details," Mum explains, "to say what kind of person we're looking for." I'm shocked that she's obviously been researching the whole thing, but hasn't mentioned anything to us.

"Can we have someone who's a good cook?" Matty perks up slightly.

"Let's hope so, Matty." Mum chuckles as we all gather around the screen.

"What about her?" he asks, squinting at the image that's appeared.

"Um, she looks nice," Mum murmurs, leaning forward to read out the girl's profile: "Eleanor Blackwood . . . nineteen. . . Oh, she's from California! That'd be interesting, having an American living here. . ."

I struggle for something – anything – to say. The truth is, Eleanor looks OK. She's blonde and smiley, but then she'd hardly be sneering in her picture, would she? "She likes drama and singing and, oh, cheerleading," Mum announces. "Maybe she could teach you, Zoe?"

"What, to shake pom-poms about?"

Mum gives me an exasperated look. "I'm sure there's a bit more to it than that..."

We move on to Sylvie from Paris, and Lisa from Germany, and Sofia from the Czech Republic ... until my head's spinning and all these bright, smiling girls start to look the same. "OK," Mum says, shutting down her laptop, "we're not going to pick someone tonight. You two are the most important people in the world to me, and I need time to choose the right person for us. In the meantime, though, I think it's best if you spend the next few days at Dad's—"

"But you just said we wouldn't have to!" I blink at Mum, thinking how quickly an amazing day can turn into a terrible one.

She musters a smile. "I'm sorry, love. I thought I'd be able to have some time off this week, but there's a patient I really want to take care of..."

I swallow hard, feeling bad now for making a fuss. So that's that. Phone confiscated, a few days with Dad, a stranger moving in – and all because I forgot to collect Matty.

I'm in my room, changing into pyjamas, when I hear his yappy voice through the wall. "Zoe forgot to pick me up," he sniggers to one of his friends on his mobile.

Yep, at just nine years old Matty has own phone and it's *never been taken off him.* "I had to wait hours and hours," he goes on, "but they made me toast and honey and I got to play games on Emily's phone. It was the best day ever!"

I hope that, if we really must have an au pair, she force-feeds him tuna mayo sandwiches every day for the rest of his life.

Chapter six

Layla

First thing I do next morning is call Zoe's mobile. When it goes to voicemail, I try her house phone too. "Sorry, Layla," her mum says. "She's gone to her dad's for a few days."

What? She never mentioned that. . . "I can't get her on her mobile," I add.

"Yes, well, she won't have that until she gets back home." While Zoe's mum is always perfectly nice to me, there's something about her that makes me a bit edgy. She's pretty tough on Zoe sometimes.

"Oh," is all I can think of to say.

"If you need to speak to her," she adds, sounding slightly less brisk, "you can call her at her dad's. Do you have the number there?"

"Er, yes," I say, feeling pretty crushed as we finish the call. So much happened yesterday – I really need to see Zoe to discuss it all. But her dad's place is over an hour away. I could beg Mum to take me, but from what Zoe's said, this Rosalind woman doesn't sound as if she'd exactly welcome a friend of hers turning up. So I'm stuck here on my own, with nothing to do. Dad's already at work, Mum's planning to take Amber swimming, there's no sound from Kyle's room yet – and it's not like he'd relish spending the morning with me anyway. I could get out the clothes I bought last week from the charity shop and try to customize them, but I'm not keen on making stuff while Amber's around, wanting to get involved.

"What are you up today, love?" Mum asks, her gold hoop earrings glinting in the sun.

I shrug, fill a bowl with Coco Pops and milk and sit beside her. "Zoe's staying at her dad's for a few days, and it sounds like her mum's taken her phone off her."

Mum frowns. "That's a shame, especially as the vintage market's on today. I thought the two of you would go together."

"I'd forgotten about that," I say.

"I'd come with you if I hadn't promised to take Amber swimming. . ."

"It's OK, Mum. I'll just go on my own."

She takes a sip from her mug and gives me a sympathetic smile. "Is there no one else you could go with?"

I consider this. There are other people, like Hannah and Ellie, who we hang out with at school sometimes, but I don't really like choosing clothes with anyone but

Zoe. Although she doesn't need to buy second-hand stuff like I do, she's always enthusiastic, which makes the whole thing fun. "I'd rather go on my own," I say firmly.

Mum gets up and kisses the top of my head. "Take ten pounds from the lunch money jar. Treat yourself, seeing as it's the holidays."

"You sure?" I ask hesitantly.

"Go on. Dad did lots of extra shifts last month, and he's got plenty of airport trips coming up. . ."

I grin and quickly finish my cereal. "Thanks, Mum," I say, hugging her, because I know ten pounds is a lot these days. I hurry back upstairs to get ready. No knickers in my drawer; must all be in the wash. I finally unearth a pair of ancient Hello Kitty ones muddled up with my socks. Luckily, Amber's still sleeping and doesn't see me pulling them on. No bra to be seen either. Typical. I must ask Mum about getting new stuff – not a big splurge, just basics. With a sigh, I pull on a dingy old vest that I haven't worn since primary school. A vest, at my age! I only kept it because I planned to dye it. Oh well, no one'll know.

Next come my faded patched-up jeans and a T-shirt that used to be a horrible porridgy colour but, thanks to a sachet of dye, is now a gorgeous raspberry pink. As I pull on my blue canvas lace-ups, I realize the sole of the right one is flapping loose at the front. Maybe I should look out for new ones at the market. Amber sits up in bed and pushes a cloud of curly hair from her face.

"What are you doing today?" she asks sleepily.

"Nothing much," I reply, skipping out of our room before she can ask to tag along.

I don't mind Amber too much (unless she's demanding to know if I *love* Ben . . . cringe). But I don't really want her trailing round the market with me. As I shout bye to Mum and set off, I realize there's another reason why I rushed out before Amber got up: so I can keep an eye out for Ben. I'm kind of embarrassed to admit it, even to myself. Some of the girls at school have turned the whole boy-watching thing into a full-time hobby. Suddenly the boys we've all known for years are now viewed as a mysterious and thrilling species, to be studied and discussed at great length. You know those animal documentaries, where David Attenborough goes into minute detail about the natural habitat and behaviour of baboons or whatever? That's how CJ and her friends view boys these days. I walk quickly, hoping I won't run into that lot today.

And now, as the stalls come into view, I realize I'm doing exactly the same thing as the boy-mad group. What would I even do if I saw Ben? Sure, he was friendly in the park, and he asked if I wanted to watch a film in Kyle's room. But then, how else would he be with his new mate's little sister? He'd hardly act all rude or sarcastic. Anyway, I have to stop thinking about him because it's just *stupid*. Zoe obviously likes him too, so that would be awkward – and it's not like anything

45

could ever happen between me and one of my brother's friends. If he had the faintest suspicion of how I feel, it'd be Death by Teasing for me. Just as well Ben'll be swamped with girls when we go back to school and will forget I even exist.

And by then, hopefully, my dumb crush will have fizzled out. . .

The vintage market has been set out in the cobbled car park in front of the Acorn Theatre, and is already buzzing with people keen to grab the best stuff.

It's an explosion of colour, clothes flapping in the breeze. A huge banner hangs from the front of the theatre: SAVE THE ACORN! POP-UP VINTAGE MARKET – ONE DAY ONLY!

Across the street, I spot Danny and Jude coming out of the old-fashioned sweet shop, and my stomach does a little flip. Is Ben with them? I loiter for a moment, pretending to check my fingernails, as if that's a perfectly normal thing to do. When I glance over again, Danny and Jude are wandering towards the market. Only Clara, the old lady who lives opposite us, has followed them out of the shop.

I must stop this. *Must* get my brain under control and stop being obsessed. Normally, I'd already be delving through the vintage clothes, my heart fluttering with excitement over what I might find. Taking a deep breath, I pull my phone out of my pocket and scroll through my contacts to find Zoe's dad's number.

"Hello?" It's Rosalind who answers – Rosalind, who made him buy hugely expensive horse blankets with special pockets for putting magnets in, which she reckons helps the horses to "chill out".

"Er, is Zoe there, please?" I ask.

"*Zoe?*" The way she says it, you'd think I'd asked to speak to the queen. *Yes, Zoe. Your boyfriend's daughter, remember? Blonde girl, shows up at your place every couple of weeks? Although, as she doesn't possess hooves, perhaps you haven't even noticed...*

"It's her friend Layla," I add.

I don't think Rosalind hears me because in the background someone's squealing, "Mummy, we're going to be late for my lesson! Come on, stop talking. Get off the phone!"

"Sorry, who is this again?" Rosalind says in a rush.

"Layla..."

"Zoe's not in at the moment, she's just gone out on my bike..." Poor Zoe. She's probably headed off on her own to avoid hanging out with Olivia. "I'll tell her you rang," Rosalind adds. "Sorry, got to go." The call ends abruptly and I feel pretty hollow as I stuff my phone back into my pocket. While Zoe has a beautiful bedroom filled with lovely things, I realized when her dad left two years ago that stuff doesn't matter very much at all.

Suddenly, he was living in the middle of nowhere with "that woman", as Zoe's mum calls her, or "the ageing Barbie doll" when she's in a bad mood, due to Rosalind's bleached yellow hair and the billions of beauty treatments she has. Sometimes we joke that she's probably made of plastic and might actually melt on her sunbed. As well as dealing with all that, Zoe is also expected to be extra nice to Olivia too. "She's been through a lot," her dad pointed out. "Remember, her dad walked out on them when she was just a baby." Zoe and I agreed that it must have been tough. *But then my dad did the same to us*, she pointed out. Anyway, Olivia's never shown an interest in becoming friends with Zoe. I hope Rosalind remembers to tell her I called.

I'm in amongst the market stalls now. Embroidered tops and floaty dresses are displayed on hangers, and wicker baskets are overflowing with shoes and scarves and bags.

"Find anything yet?" Jude has appeared at my side.

I smile and shake my head. "Only just started looking."

"No Zoe today?"

"She's at her dad's," I explain. Recently, I've suspected Jude has a bit of a crush on her. He's just one of the gang really – a boy we've known since we all jostled for space around the sandpit at pre-school. He's so easy to talk to, and Mum was right – he doesn't care what anyone thinks. I can't imagine Kyle hanging out with any of the other boys from my year. I want to ask if he's seen Ben today, but know I couldn't possibly make it sound casual.

"Poor you, all alone," Jude teases, pushing light brown hair from his eyes.

I grin. "I know. I'm devastated."

"Well, I can give you some fashion advice if you like."

"What, you?" I splutter.

"Yeah!" He points up at a bright yellow dress with orange suns printed all over it. "You should get that. It's just your colour."

I smile. "Bit too garish, even for me." Then something else catches my eye: another dress, partly hidden behind the yellow horror. It's fairly plain, fitted and sleeveless. I'm not really a dress person, but it's such an amazing colour. . .

Blue – angelfish blue.

"Hey, Layla, how do I look?" Jude's messing around and trying on hats now at the next stall. Danny appears and pulls on a crazy hat with a floppy brim, and the two of them crack up laughing.

"Beautiful." I turn away and reach up for the blue dress.

The stall lady makes her way towards me. "Oh, that's just your colour," she exclaims.

I smile. "I don't know. It's not my usual kind of thing. . ." I glance down at my home-dyed top and patched jeans and suddenly feel horribly scruffy.

"Why don't you try it on?" she suggests.

"What *here*?"

"No, love, in the changing room." She points to a

pop-up tent that's been put up on the grassy area beside the car park.

'I check the price tag on the dress. I can afford it, just. "OK," I say, hurrying off with the dress and switching the hand-painted sign hanging outside the tent from "Empty – please enter" to "Busy – don't come in!"

Even though I've zipped up the door firmly behind me, stripping down to my undies in the middle of town feels a bit weird. The tent is rippling in the breeze, and as there's no fitted groundsheet – just a zigzag-patterned rug laid out on the grass. I can see people's feet through the gap as they wander by. I pull off my shoes, jeans and T-shirt as quickly as I can and slip on the dress, wishing Zoe was here to help with the zip at the back as I practically have to dislocate my arm to get it done up.

It's worth the effort, though. As I turn towards the tall, oval-shaped mirror, I can hardly believe it's me. With its scooped neck and fitted waist, the dress fits me perfectly – but more than that, the colour's *amazing*... I can't help grinning at my reflection and keep twisting and turning, checking myself from all angles just to make sure. The dress would look great with some flat ballet pumps... Maybe I could dye my scruffy old pink ones blue to match the dress? And jewellery – it definitely needs something around the neck. Perhaps Amber could spare some silver wire and those little glass beads that she leaves scattered all over our bedroom floor ... they'd be perfect.

I take one last glance in the mirror, knowing Zoe would say, "You *have* to have it." As for Mum, she'd probably smile and remark, "It's lovely, Layla – but when would you wear it?" "Never" is the answer, but who cares. I'll invent a reason, like a party. That's it – I can put it away until my birthday. . . My mind is whirling with ideas as, without bothering to undo the fiddly zip, I start to pull it off over my head.

Straight away, I realize this'll be trickier than I thought. In fact, the dress is stuck now, covering my face. I try in vain to ease it gently upwards, terrified of ripping a seam. I stop for a moment, wondering if I should pull it back down and unzip it – but now it won't come down either. Something else is wrong too. There's a flapping noise, and it suddenly seems colder in the tent, and I can feel the chilly wind whipping around my bare legs. In fact, it feels as if there isn't any tent at all! Voices are louder and clearer, and there are bursts of laughter as someone shouts, "Oh my God – look at that poor girl!"

What poor girl? I freeze, still trapped in the dress with the thick blue material tight across my face. Has the tent door blown open, or what?

"Cute knickers!" someone yells.

"And a *vest*?" sniggers someone else as my blood turns to ice. "A vest! Who still wears one of them?"

"She does, haha!" I know at least one of those voices – it's CJ, honking with laughter now. *Riiiip!* goes the dress as I tear it off over my head, throw it down on the floor and stare, horrified, at the faces all turned towards me. The tent has gone. It must have blown away. Maybe it wasn't pegged down properly. Some people are pointing and laughing, while others look so sympathetic I just want to melt away into the zigzag rug. I look frantically around to see the tent blowing away across the grass, and a couple of women chasing after it. My face is on fire as I pull on my jeans, then my raspberry top, not caring that it's inside out and back to front, the label sticking up into my chin. Shoes on next, and I'm blinking back tears as two women and a man manage to wrestle the tent back to its proper position and pin it down. The man beckons me into it but I shake my head.

Like it makes any difference now. The whole town has seen me in my age-nine-to-ten Hello Kitty knickers and a grubby-looking vest. I march away with tears pricking my eyes.

"You poor thing," says an elderly man with a straggly grey ponytail.

"Hey, where are you going?" someone shouts after me. Realizing it's the woman from stall, I walk even faster. "Excuse me," she cries out again, "are you OK, love? D'you have my dress?"

"Sorry, I left it in the tent," I call back, knowing I should give her my tenner for ripping it, but CJ and Toni have appeared now, and are both snorting with laughter. As the word "vest" pierces the air I start running, past

Jude and Danny, who are standing in a cluster with Harris and Kyle and – oh no, not Ben. . .

Someone's calling my name, and I think it's Jude, but I keep running away from the stalls and the blue-dress lady and all the people who think it's the funniest thing that's ever happened in our town. I tear across the road, causing a car to brake sharply and the driver to toot his horn. "Layla, wait!" Jude shouts, some distance behind me. Without looking round, I keep on running as fast as I can, all the way to the park.

The dodgems are still here but I have no intention of stopping. I'm just taking the quickest route home. I pelt alongside the river, with a stitch in my side and conscious of the flapping sole on my shoe. Worried that I'll trip up – the last thing I need is to fall flat on my face – I stop abruptly and pull off both shoes, figuring I might as well run home in my socks. It's not as if being seen shoe-less is worse than standing next to a bustling market in your vest and pants. Anyway, I'm past caring now, and the stitch is too painful for me to run any more. Clutching my canvas lace-ups in one hand, I start heading for home.

"Hey, Layla!" I ignore the shrill voice behind me.

"Layla Burnett! Are you deaf?"

I press my lips together and keep walking.

"Decided to get dressed, did you?" Oh, the sparkling wit.

"Very funny." I turn and glare at Toni as she hurries to catch up with me.

"Why are you in such a rush?" she asks, catching her breath.

"I'm not," I growl. Out of the corner of my eye, I spot CJ running towards us in her khaki T-shirt, jeans and Doc Martens. Great – so now I'm in for the Jamieson-sisters experience. I glance down at my feet and notice my left sock has a splodge of something green and slimy on it. Duck poo, possibly. Fantastic.

"We saw you pouting and posing in that mirror," Toni continues. "Love yourself, don't you? Shame you couldn't get that dress off!" CJ guffaws. Obviously, her job is just to laugh on demand, rather than coming up with any insults herself.

"I was just trying it on, all right?" I snap.

"So we saw," Toni says in mock seriousness. "Oh, I feel bad now but we couldn't resist it, could we, CJ?"

I frown at Toni. "What d'you mean?"

She smirks. "Well, when we set the tent free. . ."

For a moment, I don't get it at all. "You set the tent *free*?"

She nods and slips into an infuriating little girl's voice. "Yeah. Poor little tenty, all sad and tied up. We just let it go, didn't we, CJ?"

CJ nods.

"You mean," I exclaim, "you *unpegged* it?"

Toni smirks. "Just a little joke."

"You let the tent blow away so everyone could see—"

"Yeah," she says. "Nice choice of underwear, Layla.

Won't your mum get you a bra, then? Oh, I s'pose if you don't actually need one. . ."

My heart is thudding so fiercely it feels like it could burst out of my chest.

"C'mon," CJ says. "Let's go back to the market. Ben said he'd see us there. . ."

Ben? This day just gets better and better. . .

"In a minute," Toni says, pulling a huge candy dummy from her pocket and giving it a lick. Wouldn't you think, at seventeen years old, you might not want to be seen with dummy sweets?

I start to walk away. God, I wish Zoe was here. Not to stick up for me – no one around here stands up to Toni – but just so I'd feel less alone.

"Your T-shirt's on back to front," Toni yells after me. "Can't your parents afford to buy you new stuff, Layla? Not even shoes?" Tears are filling my eyes now, and I daren't look back in case they're following me. As I leave the park, I allow myself one quick glance over my shoulder. The pair of them are giggling away as they head back to the market.

Off to meet Ben, probably. Well, see if I care. I'm barely aware of running the rest of the way, and when I burst into our house, Gran lets out a little yelp of surprise from the kitchen. "You gave me a shock there!" she says.

"Sorry, Gran." I try to steady my breath. "Where's Mum?"

"Still at the swimming pool. Won't be long now. So where've you been today?"

"Just a vintage market, Gran," I say, praying she won't comment on my pink, teary eyes or my inside-out, back-to-front T-shirt.

"Was it fun?" she asks, smiling.

"It was great," I fib.

"What did you buy? C'mon, show me!"

The beautiful dress flashes into my mind. "Nothing," I blurt out, scampering upstairs to my room and nearly skidding on Amber's glass beads before throwing myself onto my bed.

Chapter seven

Zoe

The first couple of days at Dad's, he takes Matty and me out shopping, then to the cinema and the park for a picnic, so it's not too bad. We're hardly in the house at all, and it's fun to hang out together, just the three of us (luckily, Olivia's too busy with horsey stuff to join us. Or maybe Dad just wants to spend time with his own kids). But on Thursday he says he's sorry but he has to go back to work, and leaves us alone with Rosalind and Olivia.

"Come and say hello to Popsy and Lilly," calls Rosalind, tossing back her thick mane of blonde hair.

"It's all right, thanks," I call back nervously, loitering by the fence at the edge of the paddock. "I can see them fine from here." I peer at the horses in the distance and try to look as if I'm appreciating them.

"You are funny," Rosalind laughs. "You need to get to *know* horses, Zoe. Learn how to relax around them so they realize you're not a predator."

I can't help laughing at that. "How could I be a predator? They're about ten times bigger than me!"

Rosalind smoothes her hands over her jodhpur-clad hips and flashes her dazzling teeth. According to Olivia, she has them blasted with a whitening laser every month. "Doesn't your mum have her teeth done?" Olivia once asked in a sneery voice. *No*, I replied, wanting to say, *She's too busy treating children to be obsessed with her teeth*. Rosalind also has her eyebrows done – not just plucked or waxed, but actually tattooed. A thin brown arch hovers above each eye.

"All of Olivia's friends love horses," she goes on. "You're the first girl I've met who doesn't!"

I glance down at the huge green wellies Rosalind has lent me for this glittering occasion – i.e. watching Olivia having a riding lesson in the drizzle. "It's not that I don't like them," I explain. "I think they're beautiful. I'm just a bit scared of them."

Rosalind smiles and shakes her head as if she doesn't understand me at all.

The instructor – a skinny woman who's so tanned she looks grilled – has arrived now, and Olivia climbs onto one of the horses. "Er, how long is Olivia's lesson?" I ask Rosalind.

"Just an hour," she replies.

An hour! I think of the things I could do in that time. Like run seven miles – in fact, I'm seized by an urge to do that right now. To run, I mean. To kick off Rosalind's wellies, which are two sizes too big, and pull on my trainers and get out of here... I don't care that we're getting an au pair any more. I'd rather be at home with a stranger than trapped with the world's most irritating eleven-year-old girl. And because Matty's a boy – and therefore not expected to be interested in watching Olivia canter around – he's allowed to sit at the picnic table inside the stable and play games on Rosalind's iPad.

"Are you watching?" Rosalind shouts as Olivia trots past me.

"Yes," I say quickly, trying to adopt a fascinated face. "Er, aren't you riding today, Rosalind?"

She pulls a tight smile. "Not at the moment. I have a little, uh ... injury. Anyway, don't you think Olivia's doing well? See how relaxed she looks?"

I nod.

"Maybe we should book you a lesson sometime?"

"No, it's OK, thanks," I reply, wondering if this would be any more bearable if Dad was here. When he told Mum that it would be fine for me and Matty to stay, I assumed he'd be here the whole time. Like Mum, he's also a doctor, only he specializes in bones. Rosalind worked on reception in his hospital – that's where he met her. Luckily, Mum works at different hospital, or things would be even more complicated than they already are. Anyway, Rosalind doesn't have time to go out to work any more, "because of the horses". Or she doesn't need to – now she has Dad to pay for the special

magnetic blankets that stop her horses being "tense".
Huh. *I'd* be tense if I had Olivia yapping commands at
me the whole time. . .

It's raining properly now. I'm tempted to join Matty
in the stable – I can see him in there, jabbing at the
screen – but can't face the comments about me "not
liking horses", like I'm some kind of animal hater.
Finally, after what feels like a thousand years, the lesson
ends and Olivia trots back to the stables.

Well, thank God for that.

"Matty, you idiot!" comes a cry from the stable.

"It wasn't my fault!" he exclaims. "It was an accident—"

"I hate you!" Olivia snaps. "Why'd you have to come
here? Mum! MUUUM!"

Rosalind and I run towards the stable. I burst in ahead
of her and find Olivia gripping her pony by the reins
with one hand and her mum's iPad in the other. Matty's
mouth has crumpled and his face is wet with tears. The
only other time I can remember him crying is when a
wasp snuck up his T-shirt sleeve and stung him when he
was about six.

"Don't yell at him!" I glare at Olivia and put a
protective arm around Matty's shoulders.

"I said I'm sorry," he snivels, wiping away the tears
with his hand.

Rosalind clatters in behind me. "What's going on
here?"

"Guess what Matty did, Mummy!" Olivia announces,

waving her mother's iPad in her face. "He dropped your iPad!"

"What?" Rosalind snatches it and glares at the cracked screen.

"It wasn't on purpose," Matty cries. "I was just playing and suddenly your horse was right in my face—"

Rosalind lets out an exasperated cry. "Look, calm down, everybody. Matty, that was very careless of you and – well, let's wait till your dad gets home. I can't deal with you right now. . ."

"But, Mummy," Olivia wails. "Your iPad!"

Rosalind sits down on the bench and puts her head in her hands. "Just . . . leave it, Olivia. I'm not up to this. It really is *too* much."

Chapter eight

Layla

"Speak up, Zoe," I yell. "I can hardly hear you."

There's a whispered jumble of words that I can't decipher, no matter how hard I try. It doesn't help that Kyle's still playing music in his room, even though it's half eleven at night and Mum asked him to turn it down ages ago. Amber, who could probably sleep through an earthquake, is snoring softly on the top bunk.

". . . hate it here. . ." Zoe sounds as if she's choking back tears. "She's horrible, Layla. They both are. I can't stand coming here any more. . ."

"You mean Rosalind and Olivia?" I whisper. Uh-oh – Amber's stirring now, muttering in her sleep. Still clutching my phone, I slip out of bed and creep to the bathroom, locking the door behind me.

". . . yelled at Matty," Zoe goes on. "I'm sure he didn't do it on purpose. . ."

"Do what?"

"Broke Rosalind's iPad."

"Oh, God. . ."

". . . I know it's bad," she adds, "but she shouldn't have gone on at us, saying she couldn't handle us and it was all too much for her. . ."

"That's not fair," I exclaim, and I mean it. Zoe *is* lucky, but she knows that not everyone has a massive bedroom and balcony, and besides, she doesn't get everything she wants. While I had my ears pierced years ago, she's not allowed until she's about twenty-seven or something. *I'm not having some stranger puncturing your lobes!* is how her mum put it, making it sound as if they pin you down and stab you with a needle. "Didn't your dad stick up for you?" I ask.

She sniffs loudly. "You know what he's like. He'd never do anything to upset Rosalind. He was pretty mad at Matty and then he said we don't appreciate what we have. . ." I think about Rosalind, who gave up her job about five minutes after Zoe's dad moved in so she could spend more time with the ponies. "And Mum confiscated my phone," she adds, "'cause I was late picking Matty up from holiday club. . ."

"Oh, no. . . I wondered what had happened. I've been trying to call—"

"And you know what else? We're getting an au pair!"

"What?" I gasp.

"Mum thinks we need one, after I forgot about Matty. . ."

I pause, not knowing what to say to make her feel better. "Well, things have been pretty bad here too," I murmur, filling her in on the changing-tent horrror, and CJ and Toni following me to the park.

"That's awful!" she gasps as another voice cuts through the air. "Uh, sorry, better go. I snuck downstairs to use the phone. . ."

She stops abruptly as Rosalind's voice booms out, "Zoe! What are you doing up at this time? It's nearly midnight!"

Seconds later, I hear her dad's voice. "Rosalind, go back to bed, sweetheart. Zoe, what are you thinking, phoning someone in the middle of the night? Is it Mum you're talking to?"

"No," Zoe says miserably, "it's Layla."

"Tell her goodnight then," her dad says.

"She shouldn't be using our phone without asking, Mark," Rosalind snaps.

"It's only the phone, for goodness' sake. . ."

"Well, it all adds up," she argues. "Our last bill was huge."

"Yes, I'll remember that when you're ordering horse blankets that cost four hundred pounds, not to mention the iPad—"

"The one your son broke!" Rosalind shrieks.

My teeth are jammed together now. I should probably just put the phone down, but I don't want to hang up on my best friend.

"Now, Zoe," her dad says in a calmer voice, "off to bed. You need some sleep."

She sniffs again and mutters, "Talk to you soon, OK?" then ends the call.

I sit on the loo, wondering which of us had the worst day today – Zoe, being stuck with Rosalind and Olivia, or me, with Toni and CJ's tent prank. At least having the whole town gawping at me in my vest and pants was a one-off horror, whereas poor Zoe's stuck with Rosalind and Olivia for ever. I pick up the soap from the side of the bath and run my nails along it. Things don't feel right when Zoe's not around. The days are too long and . . . well, it's not the same without her.

The bathroom door handle rattles. "Who's in there?" Dad asks.

I rip off a square of loo roll and scrunch it up. At Zoe's place, the loo roll is quilted and scented. They have three bathrooms and one has a bidet for washing your bum. But right now, I don't envy her at all. . .

"Hello? Hello?" Dad booms out. "Is that you in there, La-la? You should be in bed!" Ooh, I wish he wouldn't call me that. "Hello! Calling La-la!"

"Just a minute, Dad," I mutter.

"Hurry up, love. My bladder's about to explode here." Ugh – do other families describe their body parts in this way? I still haven't quite recovered from Gran mentioning her bunions over breakfast yesterday.

As I'm washing the soap from my hands, something

catches my eye. Draped over the radiator is a white T-shirt with a scratchy drawing of a polar bear on the front, just like Ben was wearing the day I met him. I stare at the bear's quizzical expression, wondering if he left it here when he stayed over. Maybe Mum found it lying around and washed it for him?

"La-la!" Dad is becoming impatient now. I pick up the T-shirt and sniff it. It doesn't feel quite right, smelling a boy's T-shirt, but I can't help myself. It's kind of warm, sweetish, biscuity... "Don't tell me you're doing a number two in there," Dad retorts. "Oh, hello. Sorry – bit of queue here..." Who's he talking to now?

"That's OK," comes a cheery voice.

"So, how's your family settling in, Ben? D'you like it here?"

Ben? I might as well end it all now.

"Yeah, great, thanks," Ben replies, and he and Dad fall into conversation about our town, and Kyle's band, and how great it is that my brother's made a new friend. Yeah, *fantastic*. Ben's obviously been in Kyle's room the whole time. He's heard Dad complaining about his bursting bladder and demanding to know if I was doing a number two. I glance at our tiny frosted bathroom window, wondering if it might be possible to squeeze through it. It's a horribly long way down to the back yard, and I might break a limb or smash my head open, but it still feels better than facing Ben.

"Where's your place again?" Dad wants to know,

obviously not caring that it's gone midnight.

"It's, uh, a bit out of town. Kind of on its own. . ."

"Up by the quarry?" Dad asks, obviously having forgotten about his desperation for the loo, now there's this interesting new person to talk to.

"Sort of in that direction, yeah," Ben replies.

Taking a deep breath, I unbolt the door and march out. "Oh!" I say, acting surprised. "Does someone need the loo?"

"Er, sort of," Ben says with a grin as Dad jumps in, leaving the two of us trapped on the landing.

"Hi," I croak, sensing my ears burning.

"Hi." He glances down at T-shirt I'm still clutching. "Erm . . . is that mine?"

"Oh! Er . . . I thought it was Kyle's. . . Here you go." My hand shoots out like a robot's as I hand it to him.

"Thanks. Must've left it here last time." There's a horrible pause, filled by the sound of Dad peeing for what feels like a week.

"Um, guess I should go to bed," I murmur.

Ben nods. "Me too, once your dad's finished. . ." A smile tweaks his lips. Dad's wee is *still* going.

Now I'm starting to giggle too, and manage to splutter, "So you're staying the night?" Which is kind of obvious.

"Yeah, we were just listening to music and it got so late. . ." He shrugs. Dad's brushing his teeth now. It sounds like he's trying to scrub rust off a car. "Kyle's asleep but I'm not tired," Ben adds. "Are you?"

"Not really," I say truthfully.

"D'you think it'd be OK for us to hang out downstairs for a bit?"

I pause. "Um ... yes, if we're quiet. It's only Gran who sleeps downstairs and her hearing's not too good."

"C'mon then," he says, padding downstairs ahead of me. *Don't panic*, I tell myself. *You're only going to sit and talk. There's nothing to be scared of AT ALL*. Still, my insides are swirling with excitement and nerves as I follow him to the kitchen and flick on the kettle. It sounds ten times louder than it does in the daytime, so I quickly switch it off again.

"Here you go," I say, fishing out a bottle of flat lemonade from the fridge, and pouring it into two mismatched glasses.

"Thanks." He sits opposite me at the table and sips from his glass, while I pray that my brother doesn't come down. It's the middle of the night. What are we *doing* here?

Ben brushes back his tousled hair and smiles. "I just wanted to say, I felt so bad for you at the market today."

"Did you see?" My cheeks flare hot instantly.

"Er ... kind of."

"Oh," I say dully, picturing my horrible, dishcloth-coloured vest.

"What is it with those girls?" he asks. "I mean, what made them do that?"

"CJ and Toni?" I pause for a moment, then it all spills out: about how CJ started picking on Zoe after her mum had been on TV, and how she calls me a tinker because I wear clothes from charity shops.

"That's pathetic," Ben retorts. "Who cares about stuff like that?"

I shrug. "They do, obviously."

"The thing is not to let them get to you," he remarks.

I look at his beautiful face. Even here, in our dingy kitchen, his eyes are bright, bright blue. "It's not as easy as that," I murmur.

"No," he says firmly, "it really is. Trust me."

I blink at him, wondering how he could possibly know what it's like to have someone hate you, to feel your heart sinking whenever they're heading your way. "What d'you know about being picked on?" It comes out sounding sharper than I intended. "I mean, you're popular and smart," I add. "Everyone likes you and you've only just moved here. . ."

He meets my gaze, making my heart turn over. "All I'm saying is, they're not worth it."

"I suppose you're right." We fall silent for a moment. Although it no longer feels awkward being with him, it *is* chilly down here. My parents are pretty careful about turning on the heating (as Mum says, what's the point of it being on when everyone's in bed?). "Sorry it's so cold," I say, feeling suddenly embarrassed by our shabby kitchen and bubble-less lemonade.

"I'm not cold, but I can tell you are." Before I can protest, he's taken off his black hoodie and handed it to me. "Put it on," he says.

"Erm, OK." I pull it on over my head, aware of that smell again – warm, sweet and oddly comforting.

"That better?"

I smile. "Yes, thanks."

"Erm, I was wondering," he adds, "if you'd like to hang sometime? Just us, I mean?"

"What, you and me?" I blurt out.

Ben nods. "Maybe sometime in the holidays?"

You mean you're asking me out? I want to shriek. *Me, whose dad goes on about number twos? Me, who's never ever been asked out by a boy in her whole life?* My thoughts turn to panic. What'll Kyle say if he finds out? Will Ben even tell him? I picture my brother's sniggering face. And what about Zoe? She said she's never met anyone like him. I just don't know what you're supposed to *do* in this kind of situation. Actually, I do. I should say no, of course.

"Er . . . that'd be great," I reply in a strangely calm voice.

Ben grins. "Great. Can I have your number then?"

"Course," I say as he takes his phone from his pocket. Just as I've recited the last digit, the kitchen door flies open.

"Did I sleep in? Have I missed breakfast?" Gran is standing there, barefoot, in her flowery nightie with an ancient yellow cardie on top.

"No, we were just talking," I say, jumping up from my seat.

She peers at Ben. "That nice boy's here again."

"Yes, Gran." I take her gently by the arm and guide her through to the room that used to be our dining room, even though there was hardly enough space for a table. It's Gran's bedroom now and smells of lavender and talc.

"You're a very kind girl," she says, clasping my hand with her papery fingers as we step carefully in the darkness.

"D'you think so, Gran?" I hear Ben treading lightly upstairs.

"Oh, yes. You're a good person, darling." As I help her back into bed, my mind replays the incredible thing that's just happened. *Ben has asked me out. The most gorgeous boy I've ever set eyes on wants to go out with ME.*

Right now, though, I'm not sure that I'm such a good person really. Zoe likes Ben too, and things are obviously not that great for her right now. But she'll be fine about it when I tell her . . . won't she?

Chapter nine

Zoe

While I've always suspected that Rosalind isn't exactly keen on Matty and me, these past five days have proved it. Aside from the iPad (which Dad has already whisked away to be fixed), there have been other, smaller things we've done wrong, like. . .

1. Me not showing enough interest in Olivia's *second* riding lesson of the week. "She just stood there looking bored," Rosalind complained to Dad, as if I should have been either clapping, cheering or fainting with excitement. Next time – *when I finally get my phone back* – I'll be sure to take hundreds of photos, OK?

2. Me (again!) saying I like science, when Rosalind asked what I enjoy at school. From the look she gave me, you'd have thought I'd said, "What I really love is performing cruel experiments on

live frogs." Which, of course, we never do. Or maybe she just doesn't get science?

3. Me and Matty and the Hot Chocolate Incident. Last night, Rosalind made Olivia's special bedtime drink, complete with squirty cream, chocolate sprinkles and some kind of edible pink hearts. When Dad wandered into the living room and said, "Don't you two like hot chocolate any more?" Rosalind replied, quick as a flash, "They didn't say they wanted any." Well, I didn't actually. I don't really go for drinks that look like *cakes*. "You could have asked them," he said, and the atmosphere was so uncomfortable, he grabbed his wallet and stormed out to the pub. Rosalind went all pink and watery-eyed and then spent nearly an hour in the bath.

Anyway, things aren't all bad, because we've survived – just. It's Saturday morning and any minute now Dad is taking us home. I glance at the clock on the mantelpiece. "It's eleven o'clock, Dad. Maybe we'd be better be going?"

"Oh, right – are you both packed and ready?" he asks with a smile.

"Yes," we reply in unison. In fact, we've been packed for hours. Matty's even waiting at the front door with his backpack on.

"Let's go then," Dad says. "I'll just call Rosalind and

Olivia in from the paddock. They'll want to see you off." Sure they will, to make sure we've actually *gone*.

As we drive away, with Rosalind grinning fakely and Olivia glaring at us, I wonder if it'll ever feel OK coming here. "Um, Dad," I say when we're about halfway home, "could you drop me off at Layla's?"

"What for, love?" he asks, giving me a quick sideways glance.

I shrug, making out it's no big deal. "It's just, I haven't seen her for ages."

He chuckles. "Still as thick as thieves, are you?"

"Yes, of course we are."

"Sure you don't want to go home and see Mum first?" Dad asks.

"Um, I'd just like to see Layla. . ."

He nods. "Better call Mum to check it's OK."

"I don't have my phone," I remind him.

He exhales loudly. "Mine's in the glove compartment. Give her a call." I rummage for it and find her mobile number.

"What is it, Mark?" she says coldly when she answers.

"Mum, it's me."

"Oh, Zoe! Hi, darling. Everything OK?" Phew – she doesn't sound mad any more.

"I'm fine," I reply. "We're on our way home. But it is all right if Dad drops me off at Layla's?"

"Do you really need to?" Mum asks. "It's just ... there's something I'd like to talk to—"

74

"Please, Mum," I cut in. "I haven't seen her all week."

Mum pauses. "All right, love, but don't be too long. I took today off work and I'd really like to spend some time with you." With a twinge of guilt, I realize I'm missing her too. At least, I'm missing kind, friendly Mum, rather than the annoyed version who confiscated my phone. . . She clears her throat. "Um . . . sorry about your phone, Zoe. I think I overreacted. . ."

"It's OK," I murmur.

Mum pauses. "I know I've been a bit harsh with you, sweetheart. I was upset that day and it wasn't just about Matty being left at the holiday club. . ."

"What was it, then?"

"Um . . . something else."

"Something at work?" I ask.

"It was . . . yes, kind of." Her voice cracks, then she adds, "It's all sorted now, OK? Have a nice time at Layla's and I'll see you later. Is Dad bringing Matty home now?"

"Yeah, he'll be home in about half an hour." I finish the call, and Dad and I chat about school and the cross-country team and how Miss Baker, our gym teacher, says I might be able to run for the county. It feels so good, just the two of us talking while Matty plays on his phone in the back, that all the stresses of the last few days melt away.

I've never been happier to see Layla. Up in her room,

I describe Olivia's announcement over dinner that she wants her newest horse blanket to be professionally embroidered with her full name (which I happen to know is Olivia Melody Butt, haha!). But even when we're curled up on her unmade bed, snorting with laughter, I can tell things aren't right. Layla's acting as if there's something on her mind. The tent thing, probably. Well, it'd take me a long time to recover from that too.

"Layla?" her mum calls upstairs. "Remember that thing you promised to do?"

"Yes, Mum," she shouts back.

"What thing?" I ask, hoping she doesn't have to go anywhere.

"Gran's birthday party tomorrow," Layla explains. "Mum's made the cake but she wants me to decorate it. One of Gran's friends has taken her out so I've got an hour to do it." Maybe that's what's playing on her mind. It's unlike Layla to stress over a creative project, though. "Want to help?" she asks, slipping off her bed.

"Oh, you know I'm rubbish at that kind of thing."

"No, you're not," she insists. "C'mon, it'll be more fun if we do it together."

It's not that I don't want to help. Just that I'd rather hang out in Layla's room, especially as Amber's out at the Young Adventurers' fun day, so we'd have the chance to catch up. But Layla's already heading downstairs, so I follow her to the kitchen where her mum has set everything out for us. "What are you planning to do?" I ask.

"Thought I'd make a patchwork cake," Layla replies. "Gran used to love making patchwork rugs. Remember how she taught me to sew all the knitted squares together?" I nod. My grandparents live hundreds of miles away so we only see them on special occasions.

"She can't manage it any more, though," her mum adds, glancing at me. "It's sad, Zoe. She can't remember how to make all the pieces fit together."

I glance down at the block of sugarpaste icing, ready to be tinted into a rainbow of different colours. "D'you think it'll upset her?" I ask as Layla's phone bleeps in her pocket.

"I don't think so," she replies, ignoring the message. "She still loves home-made things. She's always asking me about my clothes."

"She'll be delighted," her mum says firmly. "Anyway, I need to pick up Amber, OK? Can I leave you girls to it?"

"Sure," Layla says.

In fact, decorating the cake is just the thing to take my mind off my two days with Rosalind and Olivia. We knead food colouring into the icing, then roll out the different colours and cut them into tiny squares to place carefully on the cake. By the time we've finished we've made a complete mess of the kitchen but the cake looks *brilliant*. We have some icing left over and Layla has the idea the idea of making a little icing basket, which she fills with miniature fruit, then moulds a model "Gran" and places her on the cake beside it.

"What d'you think?" she asks, grinning.

"It's amazing! Remember when your gran used to take us up to the quarry and we'd have a picnic?"

Layla nods, grabs a couple of pieces of icing and blends them together until they're a fiery orange shade. Within minutes she's made a tiny fox, with a flash of white beneath its chin, which she places at the edge of the cake. "It's perfect," I exclaim.

"Well, you did it too."

"You did the creative bits, though," I say, even if I am pretty proud of myself too for my part in the Great Cake Effort. We hide it on top of the fridge where her gran won't see it, and are settling down in Layla's bedroom again when the front door bursts open and Amber charges upstairs towards us.

"Look what I made!" she announces, clutching a shoebox to her chest.

"What is it?" Layla asks.

"A purse!" Amber whips off the lid and something terrible wafts out – deeply fishy and possibly the worst stink I've ever smelled in my life.

We both recoil in horror and Layla makes a gagging noise. "Ugh, get it out of here!"

"Don't you like it?" Amber has plucked something brownish, like a lump of dead skin, from the box.

"It's horrible," I exclaim. "What's it made of?"

"Salmon."

"Salmon?" Layla splutters. "You mean actual fish?"

"Yeah," Amber says proudly. "We took the skin off and left it to dry out till the smell had gone and then we sewed it together—"

"But the smell *hasn't* gone," I say, creasing up with laughter.

"Yeah, it has! Anyway, it's better than using leather. . ."

Layla is up on her feet now, ushering Amber towards the door. "Take it away. Put it in the outside bin. . ."

"No," she cries. "I made it!"

I snigger and turn to Layla. "D'you want to come to my house instead? I did tell Mum I wouldn't be long. . ."

Layla nods. "At least your place doesn't smell like that," she adds, throwing Amber an exasperated look. "C'mon, let's go." We yell goodbye to Layla's mum and run out.

Even outside, it feels like the stink is still clinging to the insides of my nostrils. "Good job Ben wasn't there," I remark as we make our way along Layla's street towards my place.

"Yeah," she says.

"Imagine what he'd have thought," I add, giggling at the very idea. "Anyway, have you seen much of him while I've been at Dad's?"

"Er, he was at the market when CJ and Toni unpegged the tent," she mutters.

"Oh, no, was he?"

"Let's not talk about him," she says quickly, linking her arm in mine.

Poor Layla. The whole tent thing has obviously really upset her. Her phone bleeps again and she doesn't even check who's texted her. "What's going to happen about this au pair?" she asks, obviously keen to change the subject. "D'you think your mum'll go through with it?"

I sigh. "Uhh, I hope not. Don't mention it in front of her, will you?"

She smiles. "You're hoping she'll just forget?"

"Maybe." We're at our house now, where Mum pulls me in for a tight, heartfelt hug.

"I've missed you, love," she exclaims, pulling back and smiling at Layla. "Come in, girls. Zoe, it's so exciting, I've been desperate to tell you. . ."

"What is?" I ask hesitantly.

Mum beams happily while Matty clatters downstairs. "I've found someone!" she announces.

"What, already?" I glance at Layla in alarm, then back at Mum. "I didn't think it would happen this quickly," I add.

"It doesn't if you go through the official channels," she explains.

"So you've found someone . . . *unofficially*?" And this is Mum, who says the two of us matter to her more than anything else in the world, and blew her top when Matty was left waiting at the perfectly safe holiday club to scoff toast and honey for half an hour?

"It's not like that," she says firmly. "I just put the word out at work that we were looking for someone, and a lovely girl got in touch. I've had a glowing reference from the family she's been living with, and we've had long chats on the phone and lots of emails back and forth. . ."

Whoa, would have been nice if Mum had let me and Matty know she'd found a new best friend. . . "What's she like?" Matty asks brightly, obviously thinking this is a *good* thing. Someone else to torment, probably.

"Her name's Annalise," Mum says. "She's a friend of one of the girls who works in the flower shop – you know where hospital visitors buy bouquets to take in to—"

"Yes, Mum," I cut in. *I do know what a flower shop is. . .*

"She's eighteen," Mum goes on, "and she has lots of experience. . ."

"Which country's she from?" Matty asks.

"She's British actually, from the Midlands."

"But. . ." I frown. "I thought the whole point of au pairs is that they come here to improve their English?"

"Yes, that's normally the case," Mum says briskly, "but she loves working with children and wants to gain more experience before training to work in nurseries. . ."

"Nurseries?" I exclaim. "But, Mum, I'm thirteen! What's she going to do with us? Finger painting and dressing up?"

"I don't wanna do finger painting," retorts Matty. "That's for little kids."

Mum shakes her head. "Of course you won't have to do that. You'll just do the things you normally do, and

Annalise will be here to cook and do a little housework. But most importantly, she'll be fun."

"Fun?" I repeat suspiciously.

"Yes, she sounds amazing. She's creative and sporty – you could go out running together—"

What?!

"And when we chatted on the phone she sounded great fun. . ."

Could Mum possibly stop saying "fun"? I glance at Layla, who forces a sympathetic smile, transmitting the message: *Don't panic, it'll be OK*. Will it, though? "I really don't want a stranger living with us," I mutter. "It doesn't feel right, Mum."

"Don't be like that, Zoe," Mum says gently. "It'll take the pressure off all of us, and we'll be able to have a much nicer time together as a family." She stops abruptly and her eyes go all shiny with tears. It's as if she's suddenly started thinking about Dad again, even though it's two years since he left us.

"But we do have a nice time," I murmur, squeezing her hand.

She blinks quickly and forces a bright smile. "I know we do, darling. But I shouldn't expect you to take on so much responsibility at your age. Anyway, I think you and Annalise will get along great. Bet your mum would love someone around to help, wouldn't she, Layla?"

Layla musters a smile. "I guess so, but we don't have room for anyone else."

Mum looks embarrassed now. "Anyway – come and see how lovely she is."

I wish we didn't have to do this now, with Layla here. But the instant Mum decides something must happen – well, there's no arguing. So Matty, Layla and I follow her to the dining room, where she turns on her laptop and opens an email:

Dear Mrs Harper,

I am delighted to provide a reference for Annalise Graham, who has been living with our family for the past ten months. Annalise has been enormously helpful with my two children aged seven and five. She is a resourceful girl, always willing to get involved with lots of energy and enthusiasm. We will miss her when she leaves us but understand that she is keen to gain experience of working with older children. . .

"Why does she want experience of older children," I ask, "when she's planning to work in a nursery?"

"I expect she's just trying to learn as much as she can," Mum replies.

"But, Mum," I protest, "it sounds like she wants to study us, like we're monkeys off a nature documentary. . ."

Matty bursts out laughing and bounds around the dining room like a baboon. "She can watch me do this. She can pick fleas off me, haha!"

"Matty," Mum says firmly. "I hope you're not going to show yourself up like this when she joins us."

I frown and read on:

I would like to wish Annalise the best of luck in her next position. We are certain that she will be a wonderful addition to any family and have no hesitation in recommending her as an extremely delightful and helpful au pair.

Yours sincerely,

Jacqui Green

I glance at Layla, who's been reading over my shoulder. "So, what d'you think?" Mum asks me.

I shrug. "Well, it sounds like you've decided. What was she like on the phone?"

"Really bubbly and . . . fun."

Oh, of course. Like we can't possibly have *fun* on our own, doing the normal stuff we always do. "So when is she coming?" I ask glumly.

"We still have to sort out the final details," Mum says, shutting down her laptop and opening a drawer in the sideboard where she's been keeping my phone. "Here you go, love."

"Thanks." I take it from her.

She pauses. "You *will* try to be positive, won't you, Zoe?"

"Yes, of course," I say quietly.

"And I hope you'll behave, Matty. . ."

"Course I will," he sniggers, and I wonder what the "delightful" Annalise will make of a nine-year-old boy who still does monkey impersonations. Maybe he'll come across another discarded shop dummy and scare the pants off her? How about a mannequin's head, splattered with red paint and placed on her pillow while she sleeps? This thought cheers me up, so I grab Layla by the arm and we head upstairs and out to my balcony.

"Wonder if Annalise will like it here?" I murmur.

"Course she will," Layla exclaims. "Who wouldn't love living in your house?" Her phone bleeps again.

"Aren't you going to read it?" I ask. "You keep getting texts and not checking them."

"It'll just be Mum," she says quickly. I glance at her, but she looks away as if the far side of the garden is suddenly extremely fascinating. Something doesn't feel right, and it's not just the fact that "bubbly" Annalise is coming to live with us.

Chapter ten

Layla

For the first time in my life, I'm actually relieved to leave Zoe's place and go home. As soon as I'm round the corner, I snatch my phone from my pocket and read the texts. First one: *Hi, heres my no. Ben x* Eek! I blink at it, walking briskly and nearly colliding with an old lady pushing a baby in a pram.

Text number two: *Hi u busy today?* Ben again! Hell. What am I going to do? I should have told Zoe the minute I saw her or, better still, when she phoned me from her dad's. How would that have sounded, though? Poor Zoe, pouring her heart out after Rosalind had yelled at Matty in the stables, then me going, "Never mind all that. Guess what! Ben's asked me out!" Insensitive or what? But now we've spent all afternoon together and I *still* haven't told her. It didn't feel like the right time, either. Maybe I'm just a coward. I know she's stressed about this Annalise person moving in, and I don't want to make her feel worse.

I stop at the corner of her street and consider what to do next. It all feels so complicated and disloyal – I almost wish Ben had never asked me, or even become friends with my brother. Shall I just ignore the texts? That would feel a bit mean. After all, he's only just moved here and probably wants to be mates with everyone. That's it, I decide, feeling slightly better – he just wants to be friends. Of course Zoe will be fine with that. I tap out my reply: *Sorry got stuff to do today, maybe tomoro?* then wonder how to sign off. With an *x*? Or no *x*? *X*, I type quickly.

He replies straight away: *Great will call you xx*. Argh! Two kisses! *Doesn't mean anything*, I tell myself firmly as I march home. He's probably one of those people who sign off with kisses to everyone. I try to think of other boys who do that, and realize none of them does. It's a girls' thing, or a *girlfriend-boyfriend thing. . .*

My head's still buzzing with all of this as I let myself into our house. "Hello?" I call out.

"In here, love," Mum replies. I follow her voice to the living room, where Gran's having a pedicure as a pre-birthday treat. Mum is cross-legged on the floor in leggings and bobbly old sweater, while Gran is sitting all queen-like in the best chair with her bare feet resting on a padded footstool. She's wearing a flowery dress and a bright pink cardigan (Gran loves a cardie – at the last count, she had thirty-seven. Who on earth needs thirty-seven cardigans?). *Ping!* goes a fragment of thick, yellow toenail as Mum clips it. *Ew!* Does this happen in normal people's houses? Bits of nail are flying everywhere now and at one point I actually have to duck.

"What colour shall I go for, Layla?" Gran asks with a grin.

"Er, maybe coral?" I suggest.

"Coral! That would be glamorous," Gran chuckles.

All's quiet as Mum concentrates on clipping one of the littlest nails. "Where are Kyle and Amber?" I ask.

"Kyle's out playing tennis," Mum replies, "and Holly's mum has taken the girls out on their bikes."

I wrinkle my nose, detecting a bit of a whiff – not of Gran's feet, which have obviously been washed in the bowl of sudsy water on the floor beside her – but of Amber's latest "project". "It still smells a bit in here, Mum," I remark.

"It can't," she insists. "I put that salmon thing in a plastic tub in the yard."

"Why?" I ask, frowning.

"Well, we didn't want cats getting at it. . ." She frowns as she focuses on a particularly gnarly nail.

"Why are you putting perfectly good salmon out in the yard?" Gran asks Mum, who rolls her eyes.

"I wouldn't call it *perfectly good*, Gran," I giggle as there's a loud rap at the front door.

Mum glances round at me, still gripping the clippers. "Answer that, would you, Layla? Oh, and I meant to say – the kitchen's a disaster after you and Zoe did that, er . . . thing. Could you clean it up, love?"

"Sure," I say, heading for the door and virtually reeling backwards when I see Ben standing there.

"Hi," he says with a grin. The sunshine catches his blue, blue eyes. *Whoosh!* goes my face, hot as a just-toasted waffle.

"Hi," I say in a casual voice. *Why did I put a kiss on my text? And why did he put two?* There's another sharp snip as Mum clips a nail.

"Ooh, that was a thick one!" Gran exclaims from the living room.

I clear my throat. "Er . . . Mum's giving Gran a pedicure."

"That's nice," Ben says, his eyes glinting in amusement.

"I think you should get that salmon in from the yard," Gran adds loudly.

Ben raises his eyebrows and gives me a confused look. I know it's horribly rude to keep someone standing on the doorstep, but how can I ask him in when our house stinks of fish and he could be hit in the eye by a flying toenail? "Er, Kyle's out playing tennis," I say quickly.

His gaze meets mine, making my head all swimmy. "Oh, it was actually you I came to see. I know you said you were busy but –" he shrugs, looking a bit lost for a moment "– I was just passing."

"For goodness' sake," Mum calls from the living room, "if someone's at the door, could you invite them in? Where are your manners, Layla?"

My cheeks flush even hotter. Is it possible, I wonder, for a human face to actually burst into flames?

"Come in," I mutter, deciding that, despite the bits of icing everywhere, our kitchen is probably the least embarrassing room in the house right now.

"Is it OK, me coming to see you?" he asks, looking less sure of himself now that he's not with Kyle and the others.

I smile and push hair out of my face, wishing I'd brushed it. "Of course it is. Um . . . when I said I was busy I meant I have to clean up this bomb-site."

"You have to do housework?" He looks bemused.

"Yeah – a bit. We all do. It's just –" I lower my voice, even though Gran probably wouldn't hear anyway "– me and Zoe decorated Gran's birthday cake and we got a bit carried away."

"Right." He beams a big, dazzling smile. "Well, I'll give you a hand if you like."

"What?" I exclaim. "You could go and find Kyle and the others down at the tennis court. If you look in Kyle's room there's probably a spare racket—"

"No, honestly, I'd like to stay and help you, if that's all right."

I look at him, trying to figure out if he's *really* keen to help, or just wants to hang out with me, or a bit of both. And I can't help wondering what Zoe would think if she could see us now, already scrubbing the table with spongy wipes and squirting lemony stuff onto the stickiest bits.

"Right, what's the strategy now, boss?" he asks,

mock-serious. I laugh, grateful now that he dropped by.

"Erm, how about you do the worktops while I do the floor?"

"OK, I'll race you." We start wiping up as fast as we can, sniggering and almost colliding at the sink as we rinse out our sponges.

"Bet you don't have to do this at home," I remark, on my hands and knees now, trying to scrub splashes of food colouring off the worn, scratched floor. "Bet you have a cleaner."

"Er, not exactly," he says, spinning round as Kyle, Danny and Harris march into the kitchen, all clutching their rackets and followed closely by Jude.

"What are you *doing*?" Kyle asks, gawping at Ben.

Ben shrugs. "Helping your sister clear up."

Kyle guffaws and looks around at the others. "What's wrong with offering to help?" I ask indignantly.

"Nothing," Kyle laughs. "You two look very cosy together. In fact, I'm sorry we interrupted. C'mon, you lot, I've got that DVD we can watch. . ."

They all charge upstairs, and Ben stares at the kitchen doorway then back at me, as if unsure what to do next.

"I think we're done here," I murmur.

"Right." He wipes the kettle and rinses out the sponge. "She's giving you permission to leave," Harris yells from the landing.

Ben nods, washing his hands at the sink.

"Thanks for your help," I say, meaning it.

"No problem." He flashes me a quick smile and hurries up to Kyle's room.

Am I crazy, for daring to think that anything could happen between me and Ben, when Kyle would tease me to death? Even so, doing something as horrible as scrubbing icing off a kitchen was just . . . *amazing*. And now I want to know all about him – about his family and his life at boarding school, which he never seems to mention unless someone asks him directly. I don't even know exactly where he lives yet. *Or* his surname. I lean against the edge of the gleaming kitchen table, wondering what it is about this mysterious boy who's landed from nowhere that has turned me into a mad person who sniffs worn T-shirts and holds back crucial information from her best friend. If cleaning the kitchen is fun with Ben, what would it be like if we went to see a movie, or even a band?

"You didn't do the sanding bit," Gran announces from the living room.

"What?" Mum says, sounding exasperated now.

"You never used that sander thing to rub the rough bits off my heels."

"I did! You've just forgotten. And it's not called a sander – it's a pumice."

"*And* you throw out good fish. . ."

As quietly as I can, I tiptoe upstairs and into my room, grateful that Amber is still out. The boys are all yacking away in Kyle's room, and the movie's theme music drifts through the thin wall. I pull out my phone from my pocket and pause before calling Zoe, picturing her sitting out on her balcony, worrying about this new person moving in. And I feel a huge stab of guilt over all the things that have happened lately that I haven't told her about. But then, missing things out isn't the same as lying, is it? I call her number.

"Hi," she says. "What's happening?"

Tell her about Ben coming round and helping you to de-ice the kitchen. Tell her you're sorry, but he makes you feel crazy every time he looks at you with those insanely blue eyes and flashes that heart-stopping smile, and that he asked you out — at least you think he did. . . "Nothing much," I say. "Mum's been giving Gran a pedicure and pinged bits of toenail all over the living room."

"Eeugh," she sniggers.

"So don't wander about barefoot in here any time soon."

"I won't." I can tell she's smiling, which cranks up my guilt a few notches more. "So what time's the party tomorrow?" she asks.

"You're definitely coming?"

"Course I am," she declares. "Can't wait to see your gran's face when you bring out the cake."

"She's going to love it," I say. "Anyway, the hall's booked from three so we should all be there then. Mum's going to bring her along a little bit later so we can all surprise her." I know I'm babbling, hoping she doesn't mention the unmentionable.

"Great." Zoe pauses. "Seen anything of Ben?"

I feel my face go hot. "Er, yeah – he was here today. He's still here, I mean."

"What, with Kyle?"

"Yeah." *No, not just with Kyle. With me, in the kitchen, just the two of us. . .*

"Are you OK?" Zoe asks.

"Yeah, I'm fine!"

There's a small pause. "Are you sure?"

"Um, I'm just tired from, er, cleaning the kitchen." That's not just holding back some of the truth. It is a downright lie.

"Poor you," she says. *No, don't feel sorry for me. Not when I'm keeping secrets from you. . .* "So what are the boys up to?"

"Watching some horror film, of course," I reply. "All I can hear is people screaming and dying horrible deaths, and it's only just started."

Zoe chuckles, then adds, "Layla, have you ever met anyone like Ben before?"

"No," I mutter, biting a nail.

"You're so lucky, him being friends with Kyle and hanging out at your place all the time. Why did I end up with Matty and not a big brother?"

I force out a small laugh, convinced it sounds fake. "Well," I say, "hopefully we'll see loads of him when he starts at Mossbridge."

"Yeah," she exclaims, happiness radiating from her voice. "God, Layla. I don't think I've *ever* looked forward to going back to school like this."

Chapter eleven

Zoe

I didn't sleep well last night. Not because of anything bad — I've already figured out that, while I'm not overjoyed about Annalise coming to live with us, as long as I just do my thing while she does hers, we'll just about be OK. So, no, it wasn't that. It was the bubbling excitement in my stomach about Ben starting at our school.

I know he's two years ahead of me, but ours isn't a huge school and I'm bound to run into him at break. With all that teasing before the holidays, when CJ and her gang were calling me "Cow Face" because of Mum's plastic-surgery techniques, I'd kept my head down and tried not to be noticed. Now, though, I reckon it's time to open up and be a bit more outgoing.

I'm still thinking all of this over in the shower, enjoying the powerful spray and the fruity scent of my papaya shower gel. Maybe I could offer to show Ben around, before CJ and her friends get in there and scare everyone else off? After all, I've met him already, and we had that lovely afternoon in the park when the dodgems came. Of course, I know Layla likes him too. But she's already said she wouldn't even think of going out with one of Kyle's friends because the teasing would kill her. I could, though. . .

Going out with Ben. What am I saying? I've never gone out with anyone in my life. I'm pretty shy around boys. Me and Layla were mates with lots of them when we were around Matty's age, when everyone played together and there was no fancying so-and-so or anything like that. We used to play a mad chasing game with Jude and a bunch of other boys from our year in the playground. But then we grew up, and all of that stopped, and you only have to *mention* a boy and everyone's saying, "Ooh – d'you fancy him?" And it's horribly embarrassing. Things were much easier, I decide, drying myself on a huge, soft towel, when we were little kids.

In my bedroom, I consider digging out one of the few dresses I own, and maybe trying to do something interesting with my long, straight hair for Layla's gran's party in case *you know who* turns up. Not that he even knows her gran – but it sounds like he's nearly always at their place. Which is a bit envy-inducing, if I'm honest. Not just because Layla gets to see a lot of him, but because I've always thought of the Burnetts as *my* second family. I mean, I think Mum's great and, even though I was teased to death, I still felt proud when she was on that programme about growing skin in a lab. But somehow, I feel more at home at the Burnetts' place, as if that's where I really belong. Our house hasn't felt quite right since Dad left. And occasionally, I wish I could swap my big bedroom with its fluffy cream rug and matching furniture – and even the balcony – for a little bunk bed in Layla's room, even if it meant sharing with Amber as well. A room of your own can feel pretty lonely sometimes.

Having decided on jeans and a new stripy T-shirt, I start blow-drying my hair instead of leaving it to dry by itself like I usually do. It flies all over the place, so I have to brush it all down and it ends up flat and straight like it always does. Why can't I have an interesting mass of curls like Layla's?

I tie it back in a ponytail and peer at my face, wondering if it's time I started wearing make-up. Some of the girls at school wear it every day, but Layla and I don't bother. Today, though, I dig out a black eyeliner and a pinkish lipstick that came free with a magazine, and carefully apply them. While the lipstick's OK, my eyes look a bit too dark – but maybe that's because I'm not used to seeing myself with make-up on? I look a bit scary, I think. Not CJ-scary, but a bit tougher than usual. That might not be a bad thing generally, but is it really the look I want for an eightieth birthday party?

"Hahaha!" guffaws Matty on the landing as I step out of my room. "You've got black stuff on your eyes!"

"It's just make-up," I mutter, trying to get past him.

"Yeah, but what's the point?"

Of course, I'm not going to tell my brother that I'm desperately hoping Ben will be at Layla's gran's party. So I just roll my eyes and say, "You wouldn't understand," then barge past him and hurry downstairs.

"You look like a panda" he calls after me.

"Have you looked at *your* face lately?" I yell back.

"Cow Face!" he shouts, making me stop abruptly at the bottom of the stairs. Where has he heard that? He doesn't even go to my school. And if *I'm* called Cow Face because of Mum's work, then maybe he is too? Gritting my teeth, I march into the kitchen to find Mum. I'm glad she's taken some time off work so we can have the rest of the Easter holidays together. Matty being around all the time is *less* great, but at least he's up in his room now. I can hear his Xbox game blaring and wonder if Mum will make him stick to his "thirty minutes a day" rule during the holidays. No wonder he loved being allowed on Rosalind's iPad at Dad's. I've decided that as soon as you put a time limit on something, the person starts wanting it even *more*.

Mum's not in the kitchen or the living room, so I wander out to the garden and find her crouching down on the patio, putting some plants into pots. "Hi, love." She looks up and smiles, but if she notices my make-up, she doesn't say anything about it.

"Hi, Mum." I perch on the chunky stones that edge

the flower border. As I watch her pressing a bright red plant into place, I realize her eyes are a bit pink and sore-looking. "Is something wrong?" I ask.

"No, I'm fine. D'you think it's going to rain, Zoe?" She glances up at the dark clouds.

"Yeah, maybe."

She smiles tightly and eases another plant from its tiny plastic container. "Mum . . . have you been crying?" I ask hesitantly.

She shakes her head but doesn't answer. It's obvious that she has. "There's just . . . stuff going on at the moment," she says in a wobbly voice. "It's nothing for you to worry about, sweetheart."

But if she's worried, then I am too. I swallow hard and look out on to the garden that's been trimmed and tidied by David, the gardener we have occasionally. The grass is cut short, like velvet, and all the bushes have been given a haircut.

"Is it work stuff?" I ask.

She bites her bottom lip. "It's just . . . *stuff.*"

"They're not closing down the hospital, are they?"

Mum laughs gently. "Darling, I know it might seem as if I'm obsessed with work sometimes but it's nothing to do with that. It's, er . . . I had a phone call from Dad this morning."

"Is something wrong with him?" I ask, alarmed.

"No, no – it was about him and Rosalind. . ."

Her name sounds strange coming out of Mum's

mouth. Normally, she avoids saying it. "Are they getting married?" I ask, picturing Olivia looking smug in a flouncy pink bridesmaid's dress. Layla and I have already agreed to be bridesmaids at each other's weddings, and there'll be *no pink*.

"Not that I know of," Mum says, sounding all choked. "He called to tell me, er . . . they're-having-a-baby." She says it so fast, the words all bunch up together.

"Dad's having a baby?" I gasp.

"Well, no, *she* is." Mum sniffs and jabs at the soil in the pot.

"Yes, I do know that, Mum," I say, more snappily than I meant to. "I know the biology of it all."

"Of course you do, love." She takes my clean hand in her soily one and squeezes it.

"Isn't he too old to be a dad?"

Mum blinks at me, and her eyes go all moist again. "Well, old-*ish*, but she's *much* younger, obviously. . ." She winces as if she's caught a whiff of off milk. I swallow hard. So was he thinking of sharing this vital info with *me* at any point? It would have been nice if he'd told me himself, instead of expecting Mum to break the news. Or was he waiting until I couldn't fail to notice that Rosalind's stomach was about five times its usual size, and a mountain of new cuddly toys had suddenly appeared in their house?

A scene pops into my mind: of the one time Mum met Rosalind. "Met" isn't even the right word. Dad had taken Matty and me back home after a visit and had walked us up the front path. When Mum opened the door to find him on the doorstep, looking all nervous, and Rosalind and Olivia sitting in his car outside, she lost it. "I hope you're bloody proud of what you've done!" Mum screamed at the car, pulling me and Matty into the house and banging the door so hard a chunk of wood flew off it. Since then, Dad has always picked us up and brought us home on his own, and he never even gets out of the car.

"How d'you feel about it, darling?" Mum asks now.

How do I *feel?* Maybe she'd expected me to burst into tears, or be furious or something. The truth is, I just feel kind of flat.

"I don't really know," I mutter. "Just shocked, I guess."

Mum brushes her dirty hands on her jeans and sits on a large stone beside me. Every now and again I see Matty at his bedroom window, peering out with this toy telescope he uses to spy on David when he's gardening. I will him to stay up there and not come down and interrupt us.

"You know," Mum continues, "I've ever expected me and your dad to get back together or anything. That's all history now. . . But having a baby, with *her*. . ." She rubs at an eye with a bunched-up fist, leaving a grubby mark on her face. "It's pretty final," she adds.

I nod miserably and put my arm around her narrow shoulders. Another baby: a little half-brother or -sister for Matty and me. How weird will *that* be? Will they be like us – the Harpers – or a mini Olivia?

"I know this is a lot for you to take in," Mum adds, "and I'm sorry if I've been grumpy lately. . ."

I glance over at her, hardly daring to ask. "D'you mean . . . you've changed your mind about the au pair?"

"Oh, I think we need someone, love. We can't really cope any more, just the three of us." She gets up and turns back to her new plants, pressing soil around a geranium. I watch her hands at work, the long, slim fingers with the neatly clipped oval nails. And I imagine those hands not easing baby plants into position but working on the faces of children, putting new skin into place and making tiny stitches so there'll barely be a scar.

It's so engrossing, watching Mum's hands at work. And when I see the first droplets land on the soil, it takes me a moment to realize it's not rain that's falling, but her tears.

Chapter twelve

Layla

Everyone jumps up from their seats and starts clapping and cheering as Gran walks into the hall. She looks like an exotic bird in her peacock-blue dress and shimmery green cardie and her hair is freshly curled. Clutching Mum's arm, she looks around, delighted, at all the faces. Of course, the rest of us are here already – Dad, Kyle, Amber and me, and all of Gran's friends. Plus Ben – he showed up at our place just as we were getting ready to sneak off to the village hall, and asked if it would be OK to come along.

"Of course," Mum replied with a big, sunny smile. "If you lot set off now, I'll drive round in about twenty minutes with Gran." She handed us plastic boxes of sausage rolls and sandwiches, plus banners and bin liners filled with blown-up balloons, and we all set off.

It shocked me that, actually, I *did* mind him coming, just a tiny bit. Oh, I could look at Ben all day long, but

103

even so ... my gran's party? *This is her day*, I thought as the five of us made our way along the tree-lined street towards the hall. *It'll be full of old people and you won't even enjoy it*...Then, as we all filed into the building and started to set out the buffet, I decided he's only trying to fit in around here. Not many fifteen-year-old boys would spend an afternoon of their Easter holiday at an eightieth birthday party. And of course, Gran doesn't mind. She's surrounded by all her favourite people and being given hugs and cards by everyone. Kyle and Ben have been nominated to take charge of the music, with strict instructions from Mum to only play songs sung by dead people. Gran hasn't seen her cake yet – it's hidden in a huge square tin on a shelf – but I can't wait till she does.

Hanging back by the doorway, I check the time on my phone for about the thirtieth time. Still no Zoe. She knows we were all arriving at three, and it's now almost half past. So where *is* she?

"You OK?"

I swing round to find Ben at my side. It's funny, seeing him in a roomful of old people. He's wearing dark skinny jeans and a pale blue T-shirt and is munching happily on a sausage roll. "Just wondering where Zoe's got to," I explain. "She said she'd be here at three."

"Have you called her?"

I nod. "Her phone's off. Can't understand it. She really wanted to see Gran's reaction when we present her with the cake."

"Maybe she's forgotten?" he suggests.

"Zoe doesn't forget important things," I say, thinking, *Unless it's picking up her little brother from holiday club. But that's only because she was distracted by you, which is totally understandable really. . .*

"She might be ill," he says with a frown.

"Maybe, but surely she'd have called. . ." I glance at him, wondering if he'll ever mention the fact that he actually asked me out. At least I *think* he did. Maybe I read way too much into it and I'm just his new mate's sister, that's all. I wish I could discuss all of this with Zoe, but how can I when she's crazy about him too?

"You look great today," Ben ventures.

I blink at him in surprise, then glance down at my vintage purple beaded top, which I decided to wear with denim shorts and turquoise tights because I love clashing colours. "Thanks." I can sense my cheeks flushing. "Er, I think Kyle's looking for you," I add, spotting my brother across the hall.

Ben nods, but makes no move to rush over. I wish I could make use of this brilliant opportunity, and chat and be witty and find out all about him, but my mind's gone blank. All I can think is, *For God's sake, hurry up, Zoe!* and, *Oooh, Gran, I wish you wouldn't do that. . .*

She's snatched her friend Rose's red feather boa and wrapped it around her own shoulders, and now she's grabbed her for a twirly dance. The sight of them waltzing around the hall is making my teeth feel funny, as if bits of tin foil are stuck in the gaps. I glance at Ben, expecting him to look shocked or be snorting with laughter, but he's just watching with interest. Anyway, I remind myself, it's Gran's birthday. She can do whatever she likes.

"Your family's great," Ben says.

"You think so? They're a bit mad really."

"In a good way," he adds with a smile. "Honestly, you don't realize how lucky you are."

What does he mean by that? "S'pose so," I say with a shrug. There's a small pause, and I'm itching to ask about *his* family, but want it to sound natural rather than as if I'm desperate for personal info. "So, is your gran anything like mine?" I ask lightly.

"No, not really." There's another small silence, more awkward this time, and his expression has turned flat. What a dumb thing to ask. Maybe his grandparents aren't even alive. Dad's parents aren't, or Mum's dad – we only have Gran left. Although the party's in full swing now, with everyone chatting and dancing and stuffing their faces with food, it's starting to feel really awkward with Ben standing here. . .

"Quieten down, everyone!" Mum calls out as Kyle hushes the music. I hurry towards her as she beams around the room. "I'd just like to say—"

"Mum, don't do the cake yet," I hiss, aware of everyone staring at me, wondering why I've interrupted her big announcement. And right now, my purple top and turquoise tights feel too, well . . . *clashy*.

Mum frowns. "Why not?"

"Because Zoe's not here yet."

"But, darling, it's getting late—"

"Please, Mum! Just wait a few more minutes. . ."

Mum rolls her eyes and sighs. "OK, as long as she's here soon." She turns back to the guests. "So, er, all I'd like to say is . . . our resident DJs Kyle and Ben are happy to take requests, so don't be shy!" She beams at everyone. "Oh, and as you know, Mum didn't want any birthday presents today, but there's a bucket at the entrance for donations to the Save the Acorn Fund. Let's do our best to rescue our beautiful theatre, everyone!" Amidst a round of applause, she flits off to offer drinks to some late arrivals. Dad's chatting to friends and relatives, and Amber's showing off, performing acrobatic moves in the middle of the floor and exposing her pants in the process. No one notices as I sneak out of the hall to look for Zoe.

She's nowhere to be seen. I call her mobile and landline again, but they just go to voicemail. This is so weird – something must be wrong. I know I shouldn't leave Gran's party, but I can be at her house in under ten minutes if I run.

It's Zoe's mum who answers the door. "Oh, Layla! How are you?" she asks, not looking like her usual self at all. Normally, her short hair is neatly combed and her reddish-brown lipstick is perfect. Not today, though. Her hair is tousled and what's left of her lipstick has spread beyond the shape of her mouth. Her eyes are bloodshot too, as if she's been crying.

"Er, I'm fine," I murmur. Something serious has obviously happened, and I feel like I shouldn't be here. "I, um, was wondering where Zoe is," I add. "Gran's having a party in the village hall and she said she'd come. . ."

"Oh, that's lovely." Her mum steps back into the house, beckoning me in, then shouts, "Zoe? Can you come downstairs, love?"

We both wait awkwardly in the living room until Zoe appears. "Hi," she says flatly.

"Er . . . are you OK?" I ask.

"Yeah," she says, a shade too brightly, then glances at her mum.

"Well, I'll leave you girls to it," her mum says, hurrying away to the kitchen.

"What's going on?" I whisper.

Zoe widens her pale grey eyes and pulls a *where-do-I start?* sort of face.

"Has something bad happened?"

"Kind of," she says. "I can't really talk. . ."

"It's just . . . it's Gran's party. I thought you wanted to be there, with the cake and—"

She clasps a hand over her mouth. "Oh my God.

I forgot." She runs through to the kitchen and says, "Mum, is it OK if I go to Layla's gran's party now? I'm already late. . ."

"Of course it is," she exclaims, reappearing in the doorway. "Layla, I'm really sorry. This is all my fault. There's been. . ." She shakes her head. "Well, Zoe can tell you on your way there. And wish your gran a happy birthday from me."

"I will," I say as Zoe and I race out of the door.

I don't know what I'm expecting as we speed-walk back to the village hall. Maybe that Zoe's been in trouble for something else, or that someone in her family has fallen ill. The last thing I'd have guessed is that she's going to have a little half-brother or -sister. "It's so weird," she exclaims. "Like, they'll be *parents* together."

I nod, trying to imagine. It's impossible, though. Dad might annoy Mum with his open-mouthed snoring on a Sunday afternoon, but I can't imagine them ever breaking up, let alone having more kids with other people. No, that would be horrible. Anyway, she usually wakes him up with a poke and says, "Christ, Kevin, we can all see your tonsils!" I link Zoe's arm as we walk, desperately trying to think of something to say to make her feel better. "Maybe it'll be OK when the baby's born," I suggest, "and you've had time to get used to it."

She nods glumly. "S'pose I'll have to. What else can I do?"

"And you did once say you wish you had a little sister. . ."

"Yeah, I meant like a real sister. Not an extra person with half of Rosalind's genes, who'll grow up into the sort of kid who screams the place down until she gets the special magnetic horse blanket with her name embroidered on—" She laughs bitterly.

"And little toddler jodhpurs," I add, trying to coax a *real* laugh out of her.

"Yeah, and a teeny riding hat like, er. . ."

"Half a tennis ball," I suggest. "And a specially- bred miniature pony that's about the size of CJ's Alsatian. . ." Which actually does make her laugh.

"Anyway," Zoe adds, "it's your gran's birthday. Let's not talk about it any more, OK?" As we step into the hall, I sense her eyes lighting upon Ben across the room. My heart lurches.

"You didn't say he was here," she whispers, eyes wide.

"Yeah, because we were talking about your dad—"

We stop as Ben strides towards us. "Hey, I've missed you!"

"Have you?" Zoe asks, flushing bright red. I look at her, then at him. Did he mean Zoe or me?

"Yeah," Ben says, "and your mum wondered where you'd gone. . ." Ah, he definitely meant me then. "And we thought you must've forgotten about the party, or maybe you were sick. . ." Now he's talking to Zoe. It's *horribly* confusing. . .

"Layla!" Mum calls out. "There you are. I've been looking everywhere for you."

"Sorry, Mum," I mumble.

She shushes me with a finger, grabs a glass and taps it loudly with a teaspoon. "Kyle," she calls out, "music off, please." The room falls silent until Mum's first loud, clear notes ring out: "*Happy birthday to you. . .*"

The whole room joins in, and the back door opens revealing Dad stepping out of the tiny kitchen. He is holding a tray with the cake on it, and it feels as if the whole room is holding its breath as he walks towards Gran.

"Oh, my!" she exclaims, her eyes sparkling like sequins as she stares down at the glowing candles.

"How many are there?" Zoe whispers into my ear.

"Not eighty," I reply. "We couldn't fit that many on."

"She'll never know," Kyle says with a grin. Then Gran blows them out with a big puff of breath – at least, big for a tiny old lady – and everyone cheers as Mum reaches towards it with a long knife.

"Don't cut it yet!" Gran shrieks.

"Why not?" Mum asks.

"Because. . ." She looks round at me, "I can tell you made it, Layla, and I want to admire it for a little longer."

"It was Zoe too," I say quickly.

She jabs a finger towards the little icing figure perched on her patchwork rug. "Oh, you girls are so clever. Is that me, having a picnic?"

I chuckle. "Yes, it is."

"D'you remember the picnics we used to have? Up by the quarry near my old house?"

"Yes, I remember, Gran," I say.

"I'm moving back there soon," she announces with a mischievous grin. I glance at Mum, not knowing what to say.

"I thought you liked it with us?" Mum says, putting an arm round her shoulders.

"Oh, I do." She smiles down at the cake. "And this is a perfect day and — stop that, Kevin!" Dad is reaching to pick off the icing picnic basket until Mum bats his hand away. I want to look around to see what Ben's doing now, but force myself not to. Instead, I fetch plates while Mum is finally allowed to cut up the cake into dainty pieces. I can't help smiling when Kyle sneakily grabs our icing "Gran" and gives to it Zoe, who pops it straight into her mouth. I was sure she used to have a crush on him. She never said; I could just tell, the way she acted when he was around. A bit more edgy and shyer than usual. Not today, though. The two of them are laughing away together, then the music starts up again and Gran pulls off her best party shoes (flat and red with tiny bows on the front), followed by her socks which are more like knee-high tights really. "Don't say she's showing off her bunions again," Kyle guffaws.

"It's just her pedicure," I giggle.

"Quite right too," Mum adds with a grin. "Those sparkly coral toenails really are too lovely to hide."

People are leaving now, and while Mum takes Gran and Amber home, the rest of us start clearing up. "You needn't stay, son," Dad tells Ben.

"Of course I'll help," he says.

"Well, I appreciate it," Dad says, grabbing a brush to sweep the floor, while the rest of us gather up all the plates and cups and glasses. Although it takes ages, it's fun with all of us mucking in together.

"There's so much money in here," Zoe exclaims, fetching the bucket of donations for the Acorn.

"Shame there's never going to be enough," Kyle says.

Ben frowns. "You mean to renovate the theatre?"

"Yeah. It's good of everyone to help, but the trouble is, there aren't enough people around here to raise what's needed."

"So what'll happen?" Ben asks.

"We've got till the end of this month," I explain. "Unless some miracle happens, it'll be put up for sale and probably turned into flats."

"But," he says, frowning, "surely, if everyone made a huge effort. . ."

"Sadly, a lot of people don't seem to care," I tell him.

"Really?" Ben starts to tie up a huge plastic sack. "We should do something then."

Zoe peers at him. "You mean *us*?"

"Yeah." He looks around at me, Zoe, Kyle and Dad. "I mean, we should do something . . . huge."

"We could organize a car boot sale," I suggest.

"We've already had one at school, remember?" Kyle says. "And there was the vintage market too." I look down, trying to forget that terrible day. "Anyway, sis," he teases, "not everyone likes rummaging through piles of old clothes like you do. . ." I glance down at my purple top, which looks a bit faded now the harsh fluorescent lights have all been switched on.

"Something new would be better," Ben adds, and for an awful moment I think he means a new top, from a proper shop. "Something that's never been done around here before," he adds. "A completely unique event."

"Like what?" Kyle asks, looking intrigued.

Ben bites his lip, looking deep in thought. "I don't know yet, but something amazing. Something the whole town and all the villages around will be talking about. . ."

We all look at him, not sure what to say. The thing is, people don't *think big* around here. They think tiny, complaining about the littlest things like a few teenagers being spotted drinking beer in the park, or a swear word painted on the bus shelter.

"Shall we all give it some thought," I suggest, "and see what we can come up with?"

"Yeah, but we'll have to be quick," Ben says firmly. I glance at him, realizing he likes to take charge. In a good way, I mean. We need someone like that around here, to make things happen.

Dad smiles and pulls his wallet from the back pocket of his jeans, then presses a bunch of notes into my hand. "Tell you what. You've all been such a great help today, I reckon you deserve a treat. The four of you can go to Norelli's for a smoothie and snack, or even your dinner if you like. . ."

Norelli's? It's the nicest – no, make that the *only decent* – café in our town. I know it'll be expensive but I can't bring myself to turn down Dad's offer.

"Thanks," I exclaim, grinning at Zoe and picturing huge bowls of spaghetti followed by ice-cream sundaes.

"You can discuss your save-the-Acorn ideas there," Dad adds.

Ben nods. "Yeah, I'm sure we'll come up with something. . ." I glance at him, wondering if it was boarding school that turned him into a big-thinking person. I'd imagine you have to learn how to look after yourself without your parents around to help you with anything. There's definitely something about him that makes him different from us. Then his phone bleeps, and he pulls it out of his pocket. His unshakeable confidence disappears in a blink.

"What's wrong?" I ask, studying his solemn face.

"Uh, just some missed calls." He shakes his head. "It's nothing."

"Parents?" Zoe asks with a sympathetic smile.

Ben's mouth twists uncomfortably. "Er, yeah – listen, I'd love to come but I'd better go."

"I'll walk with you, mate," Kyle says.

"No, there's stuff I've got to get on with," Ben says quickly, then rushes out of the hall.

I glance at Zoe, and she shrugs. *Weird*, her expression says. Kyle stuffs his hands into his pockets. "Guess you'd prefer to go just with Zoe, huh?"

I hesitate, not wanting to say yes, but really needing some time alone with my best friend. "Well. . ." I start.

"It's OK," he says with a grin. "I'm shattered anyway. Those old people are exhausting. . ."

"Looks like it's just you two girls then," Dad says, giving me quick hug. That sounds pretty perfect to me.

Chapter thirteen

Zoe

As we're shown to a table by the window in Norelli's, I decide I'd give anything to have a family like Layla's. I don't mean actually having her parents instead of mine, although I do wish Mum would lighten up sometimes and, more importantly, that Dad and Rosalind hadn't made a baby *(eugh!)*. No, I mean the *feel* of Layla's family. Their big noisy gang thing, and living in a messy, friendly house where everyone's allowed to do their own thing. I can't remember us ever having big parties, even when Dad still lived with us.

"What d'you think that was all about?" I ask, picking up a menu.

"You mean Ben rushing off like that?"

I nod. "It was like he'd just had bad news or something. Did you see how worried he looked?"

"Yeah," she murmurs. "Maybe his parents are dead strict."

I shrug, trying to fathom it out. "But he stayed over at your place when he'd only known Kyle for a few days. And he was only at your gran's party, in the *daytime*..."

Layla nods. "Yeah, that's a bit weird too."

"You mean, Ben being so involved when he's only just moved here?"

"Uh-huh," she says, and she's right: it *is* strange how quickly he's become one of the family. He stays over at her place, he's part of her gran's birthday celebrations . . . it's all happened so quickly. Kyle, Harris and Danny have been inseparable for years and, since he got so good on the guitar, Jude's become part of the gang too. But Ben's been around all of five minutes, and suddenly he's one of them.

"So," I say, glancing at Layla over the top of my menu, "what if he has another reason for hanging around?"

"Who, Ben?" She keeps her eyes fixed on her own menu. "Mmm . . . I fancy a pepperoni pizza. How about you?"

I flick my eyes down to the list of toppings. "I was thinking, what if Ben's not really coming round to see Kyle?"

Layla gives me a baffled look. "What d'you mean?"

"What if it's *you* he wants to see?"

She laughs so loudly, an elderly lady swings round and gives us a sharp look. "You're crazy," she says.

"Seriously. I mean, he came to your gran's party!"

"Yeah," she says, blushing wildly, "'cause he likes being

with Kyle and the others. God, imagine how Kyle would react if he even knew we were having this conversation!"

"Well, he *doesn't* know," I reply.

Layla pulls a terrified face and pretends to check under the table. "Just making sure he hasn't stuck that stupid surveillance thingy under there."

"Oh, God, imagine!" We're both laughing so much, we haven't even chosen what we want when the waitress comes over to take our order. She struts away impatiently.

"Or maybe," I whisper to Layla, "he's creeping about outside, trying to lip-read our conversation—" I turn towards the window and let out a yelp.

"What *is* it?" Layla hisses.

"Look, there's Jude. . ." With my shoulders shaking with laughter, I nod towards the window. To be fair, he doesn't look like he's spying on us. His face breaks into a big, wide smile as Layla and I wave at him.

"Come in," I mouth through the window, while the waitress, who's clearly becoming a bit annoyed with us now, trots back to our table with her pad.

"Have you made up your mind, girls?" she asks.

"Er. . ." I look down as Jude wanders in and towers above our table, a little shy now.

"Do you want anything, Jude?" Layla says. "We're getting pizzas."

His eyes light up. "Are you sure? Don't want to interrupt anything. . ."

"Honestly, you're not," she says as he takes the seat beside her and orders a Coke, same as us.

"So what were you two in hysterics about?" he asks.

"Nothing," Layla and I exclaim, both starting to snigger again.

Jude pulls a mock-serious expression. "'Cause I thought, it can only be my hysterical face. . ."

I shake my head, trying to get myself under control. "It's not that weird, Jude," I tease him.

"We were actually talking about Ben," Layla blurts out.

No!!! What made her say that? I stare at my best friend, barely noticing when the waitress places our Cokes on the table.

"Were you?" Jude looks interested.

"Er, yeah," she goes on, "we were just saying . . . how quickly he's made friends here."

"Oh, right." Jude's mouth has set in a firm line.

"Why did you say it like that?" I ask, leaning towards him.

He takes a big swig of Coke. "Look . . . d'you both promise not to say anything to my brother about this?"

I frown, not understanding. "I don't tell Danny stuff, Jude," I say firmly.

"Or Kyle, or Harris," he adds. "Please don't mention it to anyone."

"Promise," I say, wondering if Layla only mentioned Ben in the hope of gleaning more info about him.

After all, Jude spends heaps more time with him than we do.

He pauses. "Look, I shouldn't say anything — anyway I'd better go—"

"No, stay," Layla says quickly. He smiles uncertainly.

"So you were saying. . ." I prompt him.

"It's just. . ." He stops as our pizzas arrive and I offer him a slice. "I know he comes across as really cool. . ."

"Uh-huh," Layla says eagerly.

"But I can't help wondering if he's not all he seems."

"Why do you say that?" I ask, frowning.

Jude pauses. "It's just . . . me and Kyle were talking about the first time we met him — you know, at that drop-in music session at the Acorn?"

Layla and I nod.

"He was full of all the stuff he likes," Jude goes on. "Music, films — and all the amazing things he's done. . ."

"I don't see what's odd about that," Layla remarks. "I mean, he lived in Brighton. I bet there was loads going on there. . ."

"He was at boarding school, though," Jude points out.

"They do go home for holidays," I remind him.

Jude nods. "I know, but it seemed weird when he's so secretive about other stuff, like where he lives. . ."

"He's probably just trying to make a good impression," Layla says with a shrug.

"Yeah, maybe," Jude replies.

"What do Danny and Harris think?" I ask.

Jude shrugs. "They think he's great."

"So it's just you and Kyle who are a bit suspicious?" Layla chuckles and places a hand on his arm. "Sounds like you're a teeny bit jealous, Jude."

His cheeks flush red. "Of course I'm not."

"C'mon," she teases. "You can tell us. We're all friends. . ."

He shakes his head firmly. "Look, I should go and leave you girls to it."

"I was only joking," Layla says quickly. "Here, have another slice. . ."

Jude stares down at Layla's pizza. "You only want me to stay so you can quiz me about Ben."

Layla and I gawp at him in amazement. Jude's usually so laid-back. In all the years I've known him, I've never seen him upset or hurt or angry, and now he seems to be a mixture of all three.

"No, we don't," I murmur, my stomach twisting uncomfortably. But it's no good. Hurt shines from his eyes as he gets up from his chair. He marches across the café, nearly colliding with the waitress carrying a tray laden with glasses.

"Excuse me!" she barks as Jude leaves.

Layla stares at me. "What's got into him? I was only joking!"

"No idea," I say. "He's *never* touchy like that. . ." I watch him through the window, hurrying away down the street. Layla obviously still feels bad, even when we're tucking into bowls of chocolate ice cream.

"Layla," I say, trying to lighten the mood, "what would you do if Ben asked you out?"

"What?" she gasps. "That's not gonna happen, is it?"

"But what if it did?"

She laughs and fiddles with her hair, but her eyes are suddenly guarded. I've noticed her looking uncomfortable if I bring up the subject of Ben. I know she likes him, and I do too: how could we not? But I don't want him causing tension between us. "You mean in a parallel universe where impossible things happen?" she asks.

I nod.

"Er . . . let's talk about something else," she mutters. "I still feel awful about upsetting Jude. . . I didn't mean to embarrass him like that."

"Well," I suggest, "maybe he just wishes things were like they were before."

"Before Ben, you mean?"

"Yeah." Her phone bleeps with a text. She fishes it out of her pocket, saying nothing as she reads it and puts the phone away again, but her cheeks slowly turn rosy pink.

"Who is it?" I ask.

"Er, no one."

"Layla?" I study her face and, because I know her so well, I just know. "Who is it?"

She forces an awkward smile. "It's Ben."

"Ben's *texted* you?"

"Yes, it's nothing — just about that fund-raising idea for the Acorn. Look." She delves into her pocket and thrusts her phone towards me. I take it from her and stare at the screen:

Have idea about theatre thing xx

"See, it's nothing," Layla says firmly.

I look up at her and hand back her phone. "*Two kisses?*"

"Yeah," she says with a nervous laugh, "I s'pose he's just like that."

"Like the kind of boy who puts kisses on texts?"

"It's no big deal," she says, pulling out her dad's money to pay. But it obviously is as she has to count it out twice, and when the waitress brings our change, Layla misses her pocket as she tries to put it away. The whole café seems to fall silent as coins cascade on to the floor.

The mood still feels strange as we leave. I wish we could rewind to when we were giggling hysterically, or further back, at her gran's party, when it was all about laughter and fun. "So Ben has your mobile number?" I say lightly.

"Um, yeah." She gives me a quick glance.

"Did he ask you for it?"

She shoves her hands into her pockets as we head down the street. "Yes, he did." She looks at me, and I can't ignore the sinking feeling in my stomach. Not because he obviously likes her, but because she never told me. Layla kept a secret from me, and I'd bet my life that that's never happened before.

Chapter fourteen

Layla

Amber wasn't impressed that she didn't get to come to Norelli's yesterday. "It's not fair," she announces before I'm even awake the next morning. "You always get to do things 'cause you're older."

"That's not true," I retort, almost wishing Dad *had* taken her instead, and that Zoe and I hadn't gone at all, as it was so horribly uncomfortable at the end. I know she was thinking, *Why didn't you tell me Ben asked for your number?*

And, *What other secrets have you been keeping from me?*

I sit up in bed and glare around our dingy bedroom. "I can still smell your fish thing," I say.

"My what?"

"That disgusting bit of rotting salmon."

"You mean my purse?" she asks. "You *can't* smell it. Mum made me put it outside."

I kneel up on my bed and peep through our window,

which is open just a chink. I can see the white plastic box sitting underneath Gran's smoking chair. "I can, Amber," I retort. "It's seeping out of the box and wafting up and into our window. . ."

"But smells can't come through lids," she insists.

"Well, this one can," I snap, far too angrily considering that it doesn't really matter. Maybe I'm just *imagining* the smell. In fact, it feels as if none of my senses are working properly. The TV is already blaring out downstairs (is it always on this loud?). I march through to the bathroom and start to run a bath, hoping that the hot, bubbly water will help to soak away my bad feelings.

Knock-knock. "Who's in there?" Mum calls out when I've been in there just a few minutes.

"Just having a bath," I reply, climbing into the tub.

"Don't be too long, love, and don't use all the hot water."

I close my eyes and try to relax.

"And, Layla?" Mum adds. "Gran thinks she might have left her teeth in there."

Agh! When is it ever possible to get some alone-time around here? I sit up in the bath and glance around, and the first thing I spy on the shelf is my Layla mug full of water and containing Gran's teeth, like some mutant sea creature. *Ugh.* "They're here," I call back. "They're in my mug!"

"Open up, then. You know how she doesn't like being without them." Right. I take a deep breath, climb out of the bath and wrap myself in a towel, then open the door and hand the mug to Mum. "Gran needs the bathroom," she adds, signalling that my soaking time is over. I dress quickly in tatty old jeans and a bobbly black sweater, then, back in my room, I check my phone to see if I've missed any messages or calls from Zoe during the four and a half minutes I was "relaxing". Nothing.

"What are you doing today?" Amber asks.

"Don't know yet," I reply, heading downstairs and into the kitchen. Mum gives me a quizzical look as I nick a piece of toast from the kitchen table.

"Layla?" she says. "Are you OK, love?"

"Yeah, I'm fine. . ."

"Are you planning anything today? It's just – I thought, as Dad's here to look after Amber, maybe me and you could do something? We could go to the cinema—"

"Er. . ." I pause, trying to think of a nice way to put it. Usually, I'd love to go to the cinema with Mum. But not today. I need to be by myself, to figure out what to tell Zoe about Ben. I'll have to admit he asked me out, and has been texting me, and not just about the Acorn fund-raiser. And then I'll also have to explain why I've kept it a secret from her. It's such a horrible mess. "I'd like to just hang out today, Mum," I mutter.

She tips her head and gives me a concerned look. "Any reason?"

Something twists inside me. Guilt, that's what it is. I feel bad about Jude too. What made me embarrass him by suggesting he was jealous of Ben?

"I just fancy a bike ride," I say lamely.

Mum gives me a bemused glance. "You don't have a bike, apart from that old thing you bought at the car boot sale."

"Er, yeah. I'll take that one."

"Are you sure it's safe, love? It looks pretty battered. Dad said he wanted to check it over before—"

"Mum, it's *fine*." I plant a kiss on her cheek and open the back door. But just as I'm wheeling it through the back yard gate, she runs after me with my helmet. It's not any old helmet. It's the one Dad bought me as a "present" – a dome of bright green, with stickers shaped like eyes on the front, for God's sake. I've tried to pick them off but they won't budge.

"Mum, no," I protest.

"Put it on," she commands me.

"I hate it!"

She pulls a baffled expression. "But Dad thought you liked bright colours. . ."

Haha. For clothes, yeah. A cycling helmet that makes me look like a frog, not so much. I open my mouth to protest, just as Amber comes skipping out, demanding to come cycling too. Plonking the green monstrosity on my head, I yell a quick "Bye!" and speed away.

*

It's so good being out I soon stop worrying that someone might spot me and laugh at my helmet. The streets are quiet, and to be extra safe I've already decided to get right out of town. I've no idea where I'm heading, but at least if I'm out in the country there'll only be lambs and cows to snigger at me. I'm also wondering if I can get away with telling Mum that I was stopped at gunpoint and had my helmet snatched off my head.

The sky is pale turquoise, streaked with wispy clouds. I cycle along the alley, down towards the park and up the winding lane that snakes out of town. And gradually, a plan starts to form in my mind. How about doing some detective work and trying to figure out where Ben lives? He said it was somewhere in this direction, towards the old quarry, and there are only a few houses around there. I'm not planning on knocking on every single door, saying, "Hello, does a boy called Ben live here?" like some kind of stalking weirdo. I'm just hoping that I might *happen* to find his place, sort of by accident.

The narrow lane climbs steeply away from town, then cuts in between fields where lambs are skipping about. Gran's old cottage is up this way, but I haven't been out here since she moved in with us. It makes me think of me and Zoe and our picnics, and I stop and pull out my phone from my pocket and call Zoe.

"Hi, Layla!" Phew, she sounds pleased to hear from me. I decide never to keep a secret from her ever again.

"Just wondered what you're up to today," I say.

"Don't know yet." She drops her voice to a whisper. "Mum's just told Matty about Dad's new baby. . ."

I push a strand of hair from my face. "How did he take it?"

"He was fine. Well, sort of. He started asking her how she'll be related to the baby, which was kind of awkward. She explained that, although she won't be, *he* will. And he seemed pleased about that, like it made him more special than her." We both laugh at that. "Where are you?" she asks.

"Just out on my bike, on that bumpy road that leads up to Gran's old place."

"What are doing up there?" she asks.

"Um. . ." I think about telling her about my plan to have a snoop around for Ben's house, but know how weird it would sound. So I just say, "I don't know really. I was just a bit stir-crazy at home. Amber wouldn't leave me alone, the place was a tip, it still smelled of rotting fish and Gran had left her teeth in my mug in the bathroom this morning – a bit of food had even floated up to the surface."

"Ugh," Zoe giggles.

"Can you come out?" I ask hopefully.

"Hang on, I'll just ask." There's a quick conversation between Zoe and her mum. I catch Zoe saying, "Please, Mum, can't she come too?" Then, "All right then, I'll tell her. . ." She comes back on with a sigh. "Sorry, we're having a day out. Mum says we need family time."

"That's OK," I say quickly.

"I really wish you could come. It won't be much fun without you."

"Where are you going?" I ask.

"Er . . . Baxter Valley."

Baxter Valley! It's an amazing theme park and zoo, and her mum *always* invites me, and one of Matty's friends, when they're going. Not this time, obviously. "Well, have a good time," I say flatly. Still, I decide as I cycle onwards, at least there's no awkwardness between me and Zoe any more. I picture her riding on the Devil's Loop – the biggest roller coaster in the park – and decide that, if I cycle really fast downhill when I'm heading back home, I'll experience pretty much the same effect.

I'm passing a farm now with a mouldy old caravan outside. I know it's not Ben's place, as the Frasers live there with their snarly dogs. As soon as the dogs spot me, they throw themselves at the high wire fence, snapping and snarling and making my legs work faster, even though I know the dogs can't get out. My heart pounding now, I speed onwards, cursing my bike for only having one working gear and wondering if Dad will ever get around to fixing it. Yep, that's as likely as Kyle suggesting, "Actually, let's watch a film that's *not* about some American teenagers trapped in a house with a creepy murderer lurking about in the woods."

The lane cuts through thick, dark woodland. It's

further than I remembered to Gran's old place, and at first, when the cottage comes into view, I'm not sure it's the right house. Gran had a lovely front garden with tons of flowers and a bird bath carved out of stone. Now the garden's been gravelled over and Gran's cheery red front door has been painted black. I stop for a moment, startled as a woman's face appears at the kitchen window. The face disappears, and a moment later the front door opens, but I'm already speeding away down the bumpy lane, trying to ignore all the rattles of my bike. It's a wonder nothing's pinged off it yet.

Of course, none of this is helping me figure out where Ben might live. I pass another farm, pedalling even faster now as a thought starts to form in my mind. His family are rich so his place will be amazing. And what's the biggest, poshest place around here? Dean House. Maybe that's where he lives. . .

I scoot down the short hill towards it, spotting a "Sold" sign on a wooden pole just inside the huge iron gates. It was owned by a rich old lady who hated anyone even stopping to *look* at the place, so we always kept well clear, although we were dying to explore – I remember she used to have a tree house in the garden. Looks like she's gone now. My heart quickens with excitement as I peer up the overgrown drive towards the house.

The whole building is a faded, dusty sort of pink. The house has turrets, and more windows than I can actually count. There's a huge conservatory and a walled garden, which now looks pretty wild. I bet Ben's parents have bought it and no one's got around to taking down the sign yet.

I lurk at the half-open gates, peering at the windows and trying to figure out if anyone's home. But there's only darkness behind them. Carefully propping my bike against the garden wall, I step quietly in through the gates and tread as softly as I can along the curving driveway.

There are no cars parked outside the house and the whole garden is even more overgrown than I realized. The paths and flower beds are smothered with weeds, and the oval-shaped lawn is more like a meadow. A rustling in the bushes causes my breath to catch in my throat. A bird flies out, and the garden settles into silence again. I glance back towards the gates, then creep over to the conservatory and peer in.

Apart from a broken chair lying on its side, it's completely empty. Feeling slightly braver now, I pull out my phone and text Zoe: *Guess where I am!*

Where? she texts back.

In Dean House garden. V spooky. Looks like no one lives here any more.

I wait a few seconds, flinching as a rabbit jumps out from the bushes and sits on the lawn, watching me. Zoe replies: *Mum said old lady died and house now empty.* That figures: everyone knows everything round here.

I can't help it; I'm longing to explore. Jamming my phone back into my pocket, I cautiously slip around the back and have a quick peek into all the downstairs windows. She's right; looks like it's been empty for ages. Obviously no one's moved in yet.

Then I spot it, down at the far end of the garden – the tree house. I always wanted to have a look inside. It must have been built for the old lady's children, or grandchildren, but I bet no one's been inside for years. I swallow hard and make my way through the long grass towards it.

The old wooden ladder creaks as I climb up, but feels pretty safe. From the top rung, I step into the house itself. It has a flat wooden roof and a tiny window without any glass, but it's still cosy and warm with a lovely woody smell. Sitting cross-legged on the floor, I lean against the back wall and listen to the garden sounds. There are birds and the gentle swooshing of trees moving in the breeze. It feels so private here. There's no one banging on the door demanding to know how long I'll be, or asking if I've seen Gran's teeth.

I shut my eyes, thinking maybe this could be *my* place, at least until the new owners move into the house. I'll bring Zoe, of course. I bet no one knows about it. We can share it as our own little den. . .

A sudden movement makes my breath catch in my throat. The ladder creaks as someone starts to climb up.

Chapter fifteen

Zoe

I don't understand why Mum won't let us take anyone else to Baxter Valley. There's room for five in our car, and we're always allowed to bring friends. It's not a whole lot of fun otherwise since Mum hates going on rides, even the tiddly baby ones. How can someone who sees terrible things at the hospital every day be scared of roller coasters?

"Cheer up, Zoe," she says as we clear up after breakfast. "I want this to be a special day for us."

"I just wish Zoe could come," I say, trying not to sound whiny as that drives her nuts.

"I'll go on the rides with you," Matty says, like that's some kind of treat for me.

"Thank you, Matty." I press my mouth in a straight line and put the orange juice back in the fridge.

"I'll go on *any* rides," he boasts, picking a bogey from his nose. "I'm not scared of any of 'em. . ."

"Actually," Mum says with a smile, "someone else is coming along today."

"Who?" I ask.

"Wait and see," she says, flashing another mysterious smile. For one mad moment I imagine her announcing, *Dad's coming with us. He's leaving pregnant Rosalind because he can't bear to watch Olivia cantering round and round in circles for one second longer, and has had enough of spending all his spare money on magnetic horse blankets. . .*

"Why won't you tell us?" Matty demands. Mum checks her watch, then glances out of the kitchen window as a small silver car pulls into the drive.

"Oh," she announces, "that's her arriving now."

"Who?" Matty and I yell, running to the kitchen window. The driver's door opens and a tall, thin girl with raven-black hair steps out.

"Who's that?" Matty exclaims.

"Annalise, of course," Mum says with a grin. "Our new au pair."

"She looks like a witch!" he yells.

"Don't be silly," Mum says with a laugh.

"You mean she's starting today?" I gawp at Mum. "Why didn't you tell us?"

"Because I didn't want you making a fuss," she says, already unlocking our front door and smoothing her hair with her hands, even though it's perfectly neat already. "Now come *on*, you two. Let's go and give her a big welcome."

Matty scampers outside after Mum while I lurk in the doorway, trying to mentally prepare myself for this. There's no time, though, because Annalise is being hugged by Mum, then beaming at me and saying, "I'm so excited to meet you all."

I stare at this tall girl with an orangey face that doesn't match the rest of her. "We're delighted to meet you," Mum is saying. "This is Matty, and Zoe. . ."

"Hi," I say, forcing a smile as if I'm delighted to have a stranger moving into the room next to mine, and to be the only family round here who has an au pair – a full-time babysitter, basically. I just hope the girls at school don't find out.

"Let's give you a hand with your luggage," Mum says, beckoning us over to help. From the back seat of Annalise's car comes a massive leopard-print suitcase, a red leather zip-up bag that weighs a ton, a few bulging shoulder bags and a large carrier bag full of spiky shoes. As we haul everything inside, I check out Annalise's outfit: red-and-white strappy top, tight black skirt that clings to her bottom, and towering black sandals with gold buckles that are making her wobble on our gravel driveway. Hmmm. Mum said she was *sporty*, right?

"As I've said," Mum says after we've dumped Annalise's luggage in our hallway, "Zoe's thirteen and Matty's nine. They're off school for another week so you'll have plenty of chance to get to know them." She flashes a big, bright smile. "I'm back at work tomorrow

so the three of you can spend lots of time together."
What – a whole week left of the holidays and Mum's
expecting me to spend it all with Annalise?

"That's sounds *great*," she enthuses. "We're all gonna
have such a brilliant time!" Matty stands there, blinking
at her, obviously fascinated. I know I should say
something, but I'm completely stuck for words.

"So," Mum goes on, "let's take everything up to your
room and get you settled." The four of us troop upstairs
with her luggage.

"This is such an amazing room," Annalise gushes as
we show her into the spare room. She tips her shoes – a
tangle of straps and heels in every colour imaginable –
onto the clean white bed, and throws open a wardrobe
door and peers into it.

"Shall we show you round the house?" Mum suggests.

"Yeah, cool," she replies.

It feels so awkward, the three of us trailing from room
to room, with Annalise saying, "Oh, it's lovely!" at pretty
much everything – even the downstairs loo. The whole
time I'm thinking, how long is she staying for anyway?
Mum hasn't said. Will she live here until me and Matty
are old enough not to need "help" any more, like when
I turn sixteen? That's three years!

"So, Annalise," Mum says when we all arrive back in
her room, "we'll leave you to get settled in. I thought
we could have a bit of lunch together, then all go to
Baxter Valley for the afternoon. . ."

"Baxter Valley?" Annalise exclaims, batting her spidery black lashes. "I haven't been there since I was a little kid! I used to *love* it."

"Well," Mum says, "I hope you'll be happy here. Jacqui was so positive about you in her email."

"They were a lovely family," Annalise says eagerly.

"And she gave you a glowing reference," Mum adds.

"Why did you leave?" I blurt out, unable to stop myself.

Annalise's smile stretches a bit too wide. "Er, it was just time to move on really."

Mum gives me a quick, annoyed look. "Come on, you two, let's get lunch ready and leave Annalise in peace."

"I don't like sport, Annalise," Matty calls out as we're leaving her room.

"Really?" she says. "Why not?"

"'Cause there are too many rules," he says.

"Oh. So what d'you like doing, Matty?"

He gives her a naughty look. "Pranks."

"Yes, and you won't be playing any of those on Annalise," Mum says, ushering us downstairs and starting to clatter about in the kitchen, the way she does when she's trying to pretend that everything's OK.

"What d'you think of her?" I whisper as she peers into the fridge.

"She seems very nice," Mum hisses back.

"Mum, she told you she does all kinds of sports – running and hockey and gymnastics. . ."

Mum closes the fridge door, obviously having forgotten what she was looking for. "Um . . . yes, I think she did."

"Does she look sporty to you, in those massive heels?"

"I'm sure she doesn't wear them all the time," Mum retorts in a low voice. "They're not attached to her feet, sweetheart. She probably dressed up like that to give a good first impression."

"She looks weird," Matty points out. "Her face is kind of metal-looking. . ."

Mum places the wok on the hob. "Of course she's not mental—"

"No, *metal*," he repeats.

"It's bronzer," I whisper.

"What's bronzer?"

"Stuff you brush on your face to look, er, bronzed," I explain. "But she's put a bit too much on—"

There's a loud hiss as Mum flings ingredients into the wok. "Stop this, you two. It's incredibly rude to gossip about someone behind their back. Didn't you see how excited she was when I mentioned Baxter Valley? I think she'll be great fun to have around."

"Is she gonna wear those massive shoes on the Devil's Loop?" Matty whispers.

"Probably," I reply with a smirk.

"What if one falls off when she's upside down? The heel might stab someone in the head!"

"Matty!" Mum snaps, whirling round from the

cooker as my brother and I dissolve into laughter. We've just about wiped away our tears when the *clip-clop* of heels announces that Annalise is heading downstairs.

Annalise can't eat Mum's chicken stir-fry. "Sorry," she says, wincing down at her bowl, "I just like plain stuff really."

Mum blinks at her across the table. "Well, it is pretty plain. . ."

Annalise prods a beansprout with her fork as if expecting it to leap out and bite her. "And I don't eat meat," she adds.

"Oh," Mum says, obviously taken aback. "I wish I'd known. I could have made you a veggie one. . ."

"Sorry," Annalise says with an apologetic smile. "I should've mentioned it."

"That's OK," Mum says firmly. "Zoe had a little vegetarian phase about a year ago." My cheeks redden at being made to sound silly and fickle, like I haven't made up my mind what I want to be.

"And I can't have dairy," Annalise adds, "or bread or pasta. Bananas give me migraines and I can't stand fish. . ."

"What *can* you eat?" Matty asks, causing Mum to throw him a fierce stare.

"Lots of things," Annalise says brightly.

"What about Coco Pops?"

"Er, yeah. . ."

"Sugar Puffs?"

"Matty," Mum snaps, "I don't think Annalise needs to be quizzed on her breakfast cereal preferences, thank you very much."

My mouth starts twitching as he leans over and hisses into her ear, "D'you like tuna? I hate it. Zoe bought me a tuna sandwich and I was nearly sick in the sport centre—"

"That's *enough*, Matty," Mum says firmly, turning to Annalise. "So, er, can I make you something else?"

"I'm not really hungry, Mrs Harper," Annalise says, pushing away her untouched bowl.

"Call me Alison." Mum is trying to remain bright and cheerful even though our au pair seems not to like food at all and, to make things worse, rain is now hammering against the windows.

Mum gets up from the table and peers out. "Maybe we should go to Baxter Valley another day."

"No!" Matty barks. "You promised, Mum—"

"Let's go today," Annalise says. "I don't mind getting wet." She jumps up from the table. "I'll just grab my jacket. This is going to be such fun!"

As she clatters upstairs, Mum opens her mouth and shuts it again. And, for the first time in his life, even Matty is speechless.

Chapter sixteen

Layla

It was only Ben. When I say *only*, I don't mean it like it's nothing. I just mean I almost fainted with fright when his face appeared in the tree-house doorway.

"Layla!" he gasped. "What are you doing here? And *what* have you got on your head?"

"Just hanging out," I babbled, pulling off my frog helmet and wishing it would split into billions of particles and disappear.

He grinned. "Mind if I join you?"

Did I *mind*? Was he crazy? "Of course not," I said, "but . . . why are *you* here?"

Ben clambered into the house. "I found this place when I was out on my bike, just getting to know my way round. Isn't it cool?"

So here we are, discussing fund-raising plans for the Acorn while the rain patters onto the wooden roof above our heads. "I've been thinking about the best way to raise money," he says. "What d'you think about a concert at the theatre, showcasing all the local talent."

I mull this over. "But who'd play?"

"Well, we would. Kyle and Danny and me."

"And Jude?" I cut in.

He shrugs. "Sure, whatever. We'll figure out the details. What I'm thinking is, we make it an open thing with guest singers so everyone feels involved. That'll bring in the crowds, won't it?"

"You mean a kind of karaoke thing?"

"Better than that," he says confidently. "We'll play rather than have a karaoke machine or anything naff. And we'll hold auditions to make sure everyone can at least sing in tune. . ."

"Would they be able to choose any song they wanted?" I ask.

"Yeah, of course, and we'll accompany them."

"But . . . what if it's a song you don't know how to play?"

He shrugs. "It won't be."

"Really? You can play *anything*?"

"Yeah, pretty much, and I'm sure Kyle and Danny can too." He smiles, his eyes gleaming in the sliver of light that's coming in through the window. He's so confident – he seems to think anything's possible if you want it enough. "Anyway," Ben goes on, "it wouldn't be about the band. The focus will be on the singers – that's what'll make people come. They'll want to see their son or daughter singing, won't they? And everyone else will be desperate to see how it all turns out. . ." I nod, starting to picture it now. "You'd do it, wouldn't you?" he asks. "Kyle says you and Zoe are always singing in your room. . ."

"*Were*," I correct him, "till he recorded us and teased us to death. . ."

"Yeah." He grins. "He played it to me."

"He didn't!" I shriek, my cheeks burning.

He touches my arm reassuringly, causing sparks to shoot up its entire length. "Don't be embarrassed. You both have great voices. . ."

I shake my head, pretty certain that I won't be singing onstage in front of Ben any time soon. "Listen," I say, "it's stopped raining. Guess I'd better head home."

"Me too," he says. We clamber down the ladder to where Ben's bike is lying on its side in the long, wet grass. Amazingly, it's even more wrecked than mine. Its spokes are bent, some are held together with tape, and there's more thick silver tape wound around the broken mudguard. He looks embarrassed when he sees me glancing down at it, so I decide not to comment on it. He picks up a rucksack that was lying beside it, and slings it onto his back.

"What's in there?" I ask.

"Er, just shopping. Food and stuff."

"You mean for your family? You have to do the shopping on your bike?"

Ben shrugs. "It's fine. It's not heavy."

"But couldn't your mum or dad—" I start.

"Oh, I don't mind doing it," he says quickly. "Anyway, I really hope you'll sing at the concert. You and Zoe should pick a song each. Or would that be weird? After all, it could get pretty competitive. . ." And with that, he cycles off, whizzing along the twisty lane.

I watch him growing smaller, wondering what on earth he meant. I've *never* felt competitive with Zoe. I don't care that she's a brilliant runner and the best at science and has tons more stuff than me, because she's my best friend in the world. . . Yet I haven't told her about the biggest secret of my life, have I? And it feels like this secret of mine is growing bigger by the day.

I cycle home, my bike rattling like crazy along the bumpy track. It's only when I reach my front door that I realize my frog helmet is still lying in the tree house.

Chapter seventeen

Zoe

We are on the Devil's Loop, Annalise and me, zooming upside down then climbing the long, slow hill and pausing for an agonizing moment before our car creeps over the top. It charges down, flying around twists and turns and finally comes to an abrupt halt.

"That was great," she exclaims. "Let's have another go!"

"I think I'll go on something else," I say, catching my breath and looking around for Matty, who's at the shooting game with Mum. He's already been on the Loop four times with Annalise and me, and finally said he felt sick. I do too. I mean, I *love* this ride. But, come on ... five times? My stir-fry is swirling about in my stomach and I'm so dizzy I have to grip the railings as we make our way off the ride.

"Oh, come on," Annalise insists. "Don't you like it?"

"Course I do," I say, focusing on the little black smears

where her mascara has run in the rain. "I just feel a bit queasy. Maybe later. . ."

"But your mum's bought us day tickets. We can go on everything as much as we want!"

"I'll be sick if I do, honestly." I'm trying to be nice to her, but she's so *pushy*.

"You're no fun," she announces. With a resigned shrug, I head towards Matty and Mum. She's encouraging him to take aim slowly and focus on the centre of the target.

"You could win that big fluffy monkey," Annalise says, plonking a hand on her hip.

Pow – he shoots the bullseye. "Did it!" he screams.

"Well done, Matty," Mum says, all smiles.

The stall man wanders over and grins. "Choose whatever you like, son."

"Get the monkey," Annalise says, at which Matty swings around to face her.

"I don't want the monkey. I'm not a baby, y'know—"

"Matty," Mum exclaims, "that's so rude."

Matty scowls and points at a row of clear plastic bags hanging at the side of the stall, each containing a goldfish.

"No," Mum groans. "Not another fish—"

"Please, Mum," Matty wails. "You said I could get another!"

Considering this is supposed to be a fun day out, Mum's starting to look pretty stressed. "You were so sad when Jaws died, Matty," she reminds him. "You cried for a whole day."

"Yeah," he counters, "but that's 'cause a cat got in our house and ate him. That wouldn't happen again. We'd keep the windows closed."

Mum sighs loudly. "I know, love, but these goldfish don't usually live for long and I'd hate to see you all upset again." She turns to Annalise. "It was the neighbours' cat..."

"Oh dear," she says, stifling a yawn, then pulls out a tiny mirror from her shoulder bag, wets a finger and wipes away the mascara smudges

"I came up to my room," Matty goes on, "and Jaws was half-eaten on the carpet with his guts out—"

"OK, just get the fish," Mum says quickly, smiling tightly as the stall man hands her a plastic bag.

Matty's thrilled with his prize as we make for the picnic area. "I'm gonna call him Fanta," he announces.

"Great name," Mum says, producing apples, cereal bars and bottles of water from her bag. "Will you have something, Annalise? Don't want you fading away."

Annalise glances at the snacks. "No, thanks. I'm gonna buy some doughnuts. Anyone else want some?"

"No, thank you," Mum says, answering for Matty and me. She *hates* fairground food. The one time she gave in and bought me a candyfloss – the time Matty won Jaws – she made me clean my teeth for a full five minutes when we got home.

We watch Annalise stride away to the doughnut kiosk. "Mum, she's not quite what I expected," I murmur.

"I'm sure she's trying to be friendly," Mum says. "Anyway, she's only just arrived and she's probably nervous – wouldn't you be, if you were suddenly thrown together with a family you'd never met before?"

"Yes, but—" I start.

"She's coming back," Mum says quickly, and even though she greets Annalise with a wide smile, I can tell she's not completely sure about her, either. Especially when she buys *another* bag of doughnuts, plus some neon-yellow marshmallow sweets, which she scoffs all by herself.

For the rest of the afternoon, Mum waits patiently, sitting on a bench and sipping cup after cup of coffee whilst Matty and I go on the water slide, the big wheel and some of the tamer rides. Annalise spends the whole of the time on the Devil's Loop.

"She's having more doughnuts!" Matty announces, pointing as she devours her snack in the queue. Later, we spot her with an enormous pink cloud of candyfloss, then sucking on a giant stick of rock as she waits for her seventh go on the Loop.

"We really must go," Mum says when we check back in. "The park's closing soon. . . Have either of you seen Annalise?"

"Nah," Matty says.

"Me neither," I say. It's starting to rain again now, and the sky has turned stormy grey.

"I hope she's all right," Mum says as we start to search for her.

"Of course she is, Mum," I try to reassure her. "She's eighteen. I'm sure she can take care of herself."

That's when I spot her, wobbling towards us in her towering heels. Her black hair's all straggly and her red lipstick is smeared, and her face is literally a startling shade of green.

"Annalise!" Mum cries, hurrying towards her. "What happened to you?"

"Feel sick," she mutters, clasping a hand to her stomach.

"Oh, you poor girl. Let's get you home."

"Sorry," she groans as we head for our car.

"Don't worry," Mum tells her. "All that matters is that you're OK. Will you be all right on the drive home, d'you think?"

She nods miserably, and we all climb into the car. Matty and I exchange looks on the back seat as Mum pulls out of the car park. "Poor you," she says again. "I feel so *responsible*. . ." Hang on – it wasn't Mum who forced her to eat all those doughnuts and sweets and then go on a roller coaster a million times, was it? Annalise has her head in her hands now, and Mum's so distracted by constantly glancing at her that the car behind us beeps at us.

"Mum," I say, "the traffic lights have turned green. . ."

"Ooops," she says, adding, "Maybe you'd better go to bed when we get home, Annalise. You do look terrible."

"I'll be all right," Annalise mutters, then there's a

terrible splattering noise as she's sick all down her front.

"Oh, God," Mum cries. "I'll stop as soon as I can—"

"Ugh, that stinks!" Matty announces.

"Yes, thank you, Matty," Mum snaps, like any of this is his fault. His face crumples and he grips the top of his goldfish bag. *Hey*, I whisper to him as Mum pulls into a lay-by, *it's all right.*

Is it really, though? I'm still wondering when Annalise pukes again, on our stair carpet and the landing, before tumbling into bed.

"What a day!" Mum says, sinking onto the sofa between Matty and me, after clearing up the mess.

"I don't like her," Matty growls.

"Come on, darling," she says gently, "I'm sure she's a perfectly nice girl. Everyone gets sick sometimes."

Mum smiles at me, but I see a flicker of worry in her eyes. She puts an arm around me, and I snuggle closer, glad it's just the three of us here. I know Annalise has only been here for one day, but things already feel different and I don't like it one bit.

Chapter eighteen

Layla

Zoe isn't allowed to come over during the next few days. "Mum says it's our chance to get to know Annalise," she says glumly, so I hang out with Mum and Amber and Gran, and try not to think of my Easter holidays slipping away. Things look up on Thursday, when I hear Danny, Jude and Harris arriving, and I assume that Ben will turn up soon to join them. But when Kyle ushers the boys up to his room, it's clear that he hasn't been invited today.

"He's only just moved here and he wants to organize a concert?" That's Danny's voice I can hear through my bedroom wall. "That's a bit weird."

"It's not a bad idea," Jude offers. "If no one raises enough money soon, the Acorn will close and then where are we going to rehearse?"

"It does seem a bit much, though," Kyle adds. "Like he's trying to take over."

"Yeah," Danny says. "I mean, he's great and all that. I like having him around. But it's almost as if no one else gets a say in what we do any more." It's Friday afternoon and the four boys are grumbling away in Kyle's room. As usual, I can hear every word.

"And we don't really need anyone new in the band," Harris adds. "Jude's our guitarist.

"You're not even in it," Danny teases him. "You don't play anything—"

"I help, don't I?" he retorts. "I come up with ideas for songs—"

"Ben *is* a brilliant guitarist, though," Kyle points out.

"Yeah," Jude agrees. "I s'pose we've just got to put up with him trying to organize us all." I'm wondering how Jude really feels about this. He might be a younger, but he never misses a rehearsal. Sometimes, I suspect he's the one who takes the band most seriously. And if Ben joins permanently, will there still be a place for him?

"Ben doesn't even know our songs," Danny points out.

"Well, he did come to a rehearsal," Kyle reminds him.

"Yeah, but not to listen to us. He just wanted to play his own stuff, remember?"

"His songs are pretty good," Jude adds.

"Are you saying ours aren't?" snaps Danny, in that bossy, big-brotherly way he has sometimes.

"No, of course not—"

"We've been together for years and he's gonna barge

in and change everything?" That's Danny again, and in some ways he's right.

Ben *has* changed everything. The boys never used to bicker like this; I don't think I've ever heard them argue in all the years they've been friends. And something's come between me and Zoe too. I haven't even told her about hanging out with Ben in the tree house up at Dean House. Plus things aren't the same for me, either. I can't seem to concentrate these days. I can't read or draw or finish stitching the multi-coloured braid onto the denim shorts I found in the charity shop, or do any of the things I used to love doing. I could call Zoe, but no doubt she's out yet again with Annalise. I hope she's not always this busy. New term starts on Monday and her mum's not keen on her hanging out at my place after school because she reckons she should spend about eight hundred hours a night doing homework.

There's a knock on the door followed by a silence in Kyle's room.

"Can't anyone answer the door around here?" Mum calls out downstairs to no one in particular. Then, "Oh, hello, Ben. The boys are in Kyle's room – just head up. . . And, Layla? Come here a minute, love! I want to go through your school uniform with you, make sure you're all sorted for next term. . ."

I groan and head for the door.

"Hey," Ben says with a big grin as we meet on the landing.

155

"Hey," I reply awkwardly.

"Just here to talk to the guys about the concert. . ."

I force a smile. "Great. . ." Has he any idea that they're finding him a bit pushy? Probably not. I've never met anyone so confident and sure of himself before.

"It's going to be brilliant," he adds. "You will take part, won't you?"

"Yeah, of course," I say, hurrying downstairs.

In the kitchen, Mum has spread out all my school clothes on the table. "That time of year again," she says, giving me a wry smile. Last term, she means. Which basically translates as: *OK, so you've just about grown out of everything but can we possibly get through to the summer holidays without having to buy anything new?* I pick up a grey skirt that would just about fit a hamster, and a V-necked sweater that's not just bobbly, it's virtually *all* bobble.

"Mum, it all looks a bit tragic," I murmur. "I did tell you that when we broke up."

She sighs. "I know, sweetheart. We should have gone shopping at the start of the holidays. . ."

"You're lucky." I swing round to see Jude in the kitchen doorway, clutching his guitar. "Mum still tries to force me into Danny's old cast-offs."

I smile at him, pleased that he doesn't seem annoyed any more, like he was when he marched out of Norelli's. I'm also wondering what's happening up in Kyle's room. "Yeah, well – I s'pose this lot'll do me as long as I stop growing," I add with a shrug.

He chuckles, then says, "Anyway, I'm off," and makes for the door.

"I thought you were planning this fund-raising thing?" I call after him.

"Well, *they* are," he says with a roll of his eyes. "At least, they're trying to."

I blink at him. "It all sounded a bit heated up there." I pause. "Sorry, I couldn't help overhearing. . ."

"That's OK." His eyes meet mine. "But you're right – it's ended up with everyone bickering. . ."

"Because of Ben?" I ask.

"Yeah." Jude shrugs. "You know what we're like. We've always agreed on pretty much everything, and it's been *everyone's* band – like, there's no boss. . ."

I nod, glad that he feels he can talk to me. "And now," I suggest, "there *is* a boss."

"Yep. It's just not the same, Layla. Everyone's falling out because Ben wants us to drop all our songs and play his, which is fine, they're really good, but he's going to do all the guitar solos too—"

"What does Kyle think?" I cut in.

"He said it's not happening, that everyone has to agree – but you know what Ben's like. . ."

My face flushes pink. "Yeah."

"He kind of gets what he wants."

There's an awkward pause and I glance down at my feet. "So," I say hesitantly, "what about you? I mean . . . *you* do the solos, don't you?"

We're standing in the doorway now, and Kyle appears on the stairs. "Jude, don't be like this," he mutters. "Don't storm off."

Jude looks up at my brother, determination shining from his eyes. "I'm not storming anywhere."

"Yeah, you are—"

"I told you," Jude interrupts, "it's been brilliant. Being in the band's the best thing I've ever done. But you know what? Once it stops being fun, I'm out."

"But you can't!" Kyle exclaims. "We *need* you."

"Yes, I can," Jude says firmly. "There are other people I can play with. Maybe it's time for a change anyway." He turns away from Kyle, and his eyes meet mine briefly, then he slings his guitar onto his back and strolls off down the street as if he hasn't a care in the world.

Chapter nineteen

Zoe

Saturday morning, and Mum's left instructions for Annalise to take us bowling today. It's her sixth day here and we've barely spent a minute in the house. Every morning Mum's handed Annalise a wad of money and said, "Have a lovely day!" before rushing off to work. We've been to the cinema twice, the ice rink and the swimming pool *three times*. Actually, Annalise didn't come into any of those places with us. She just dropped us off in her little silver car then picked us up a few hours later. I'm not sure if Mum's just desperate for us to like Annalise, and thinks that the more "fun" things we do, the more we'll agree that she's "a lovely, bright, bubbly girl". Or maybe it's for Annalise's benefit, so she doesn't get bored living in a small, sleepy town. Normally, I'd love to do all these things – *with Layla*. And every time I politely asked if she could come along too, Mum just looked hassled and said, "Oh, I think that'd be a bit much for Annalise." As if Layla's five, and is likely to run into the road or throw a tantrum. "We'd better go soon," Annalise announces, clomping into the kitchen in her towering red shoes, a strappy white top and the short black skirt that clings to her bum.

"I'm still having my breakfast," Matty grumbles.

She stands over him, sighing impatiently. Her top has the word "dazzle" on the front, picked out in silvery sparkles.

"Are you going to come bowling with us?" I ask, lacing up my own trainers.

"Of course not," she exclaims.

I look up at her. "Why not?"

She sniffs loudly. "I'm not wearing those horrible shoes for anyone."

Matty stares at her. "You mean *bowling* shoes?"

"Yeah."

"But . . . what about when you do sport?" I venture.

She frowns, as if she's struggling to know how to respond. "I've got trainers," she mutters, removing Matty's bowl of muesli from the table.

"Hey – I hadn't finished that," he yells.

"Hard luck. . ."

"Annalise—" I start, wishing Mum was here to see this. So far, when we've all been at home, Annalise has pretty much stayed in her room. When she's been driving us places, she's been too busy muttering and swearing at other drivers to pay much attention to us. She was nice enough for the first few days but now it's as if the real person is starting to show through.

"You don't have trainers," Matty announces, getting up from his chair and marching to the bin. He stamps on the pedal to open it and peers in at the remains of his breakfast.

"What are you talking about?" she says with a nasty laugh. "And what are you planning to do with the cereal – spoon it back out and eat it?"

"Don't be so horrible," I snap. "He hasn't done anything to you." My cheeks are blazing now.

Matty turns to me. "She doesn't have trainers 'cause I've been in her room and looked. *All* her shoes are like that—" He points at the red stilettos.

"What were you doing in my room?" Her eyes are wide now, her mouth set in a scowl.

"It's *our* house," he says firmly. I grab him by the hand and pull him out into the hallway.

"Matty, don't be like this," I hiss. "We've *got* to try and get on with her."

"Why?"

"Because of Mum. . ."

We fall silent as Annalise strides out of the kitchen. "C'mon on, you two," she says with a sigh. "Let's just go to the bowling alley."

As we drive away from our house, I wonder if we're being too harsh on her. I mean, I hate it when Matty pokes about in my bedroom too. Maybe Mum's right, and it's tough for Annalise, trying to fit in with a new family. I decide to test her, to see if she's capable of being nice. "Er . . . Annalise," I say hesitantly, "would it be OK if my friend Layla comes with us?"

She gives me a quick glance in the mirror. Matty and I are on the back seat; her shiny red handbag must have the passenger seat to itself. "I don't see why not," she murmurs. "Where does she live?"

"Turn right at the traffic lights," I say, my heart soaring, despite Matty grumbling that *he* wants to bring a friend too, and that of course there's room in the car because we could all squish up. "Just here," I say, leaping out of the car the moment she pulls up in front of Layla's house.

It's Layla who answers the door. "Want to come bowling?" I ask.

"What, now? Yeah, why not?! Give me a sec and I'll get my coat."

As Layla squeezes onto the back seat with us, I have a feeling today will be more fun than I thought.

In fact, bowling is brilliant. We have tons of goes, and Mum gave us money for snacks, even though she views bowling-alley food in the same way as fairground doughnuts – i.e. *bad for us*. So when our time's up in the alley, we install ourselves in the café and order plates of chips. I fill Layla in on the events of the past few days, and then it's Matty's turn.

"I hate her," he mutters, stuffing chips into his mouth the minute they arrive.

"Why? Layla asks.

"She threw my breakfast in the bin."

"What?" she exclaims.

"She's just a bit snappy and she obviously doesn't like us that much," I add.

Layla frowns. "What are you gonna do?"

I sip my coke and, as soon as Matty's finished eating, hand him a fistful of coins to go away and play the video games. "Guess there's nothing I can do. I just hope Mum's not expecting her to take us out all the time. I feel like I've hardly seen you."

Layla nods. "Things have been weird at our house too."

"What's been happening?"

"Um . . . well, Ben's had an idea to raise funds for the Acorn. He wants to do a concert. . ."

"What, all by himself?"

"No, he's sort of muscled into Kyle's band," she explains. "He came round this morning—"

"He was at your house when we picked you up?" I shriek. "Why didn't you say?"

She laughs. "It's hardly unusual these days. Anyway, before he showed up, the boys were saying they're sick of him trying to take over. Then Jude left. It looks like Ben's replaced him. . ."

"That's not fair! Jude's played with them right from the start."

Layla shrugs. "I know. He just said it's no fun any more, and that he'll find himself another band."

I pause, mulling this over. "Have you asked Kyle what's going on?"

"No. Guess it's none of my business really. . ."

Matty wanders back, asking for more money, but it's time to go. As we leave the bowling alley we spot Annalise sitting in her little silver car in the car park, throwing sweet wrappers out of the window.

Without asking, Matty opens the front passenger door, plonks her handbag onto the floor and scrambles onto the seat beside her.

She glares at him but doesn't say anything.

"Erm, Annalise," I say from the back, "could we put these bags of shopping in the boot? It's a bit of a squash. . ." Three bulging carrier bags have been plonked in the middle of the seat. I peer into them; looks like all crisps, biscuits and sweets.

"Nah, they're all right there," she says, pulling out of the parking space as Layla and I exchange a look.

"What's it all for?" I ask.

Annalise laughs. "To eat, of course. Sorry, Zoe, but I can't be doing with the stuff your mum cooks. I'm gonna *starve* unless I get myself something decent to eat."

Layla and I are sniggering now. Taking care not to rustle the bags, I open them up slightly so Layla can see all the Oreos, Kit Kats and bumper packs of Hula Hoops.

Annalise's mobile rings. Even though she's driving, she answers it. "Hi, Daddy, how are you?" *Daddy?* Her voice is different: posher, like she's suddenly switched to best behaviour. I glance at Layla as Annalise drives one-handed, clutching the phone to her ear.

"It's against the law to use a mobile when you're driving," Matty says, but she ignores him.

"Yes, Daddy – it's going really well," she says, in the new voice we've never heard before. "I promise. Yes, of course, I remember what you said." She nods while he chats some more. "No, that won't ever happen again. Honestly, Daddy. They *love* me. They've already said I'm the best au pair they've ever had. . ."

"But we haven't had any others!" Matty yells. While Annalise chatters on as if he hadn't spoken, I gawp at Layla, who gives me a *what's-she-on-about?* look. Finally, she finishes the call.

"You're the only au pair we've had," Matty reminds her, "so how come you're the best?"

"I just am," she says with a snort.

"And why did you talk to your dad in that funny voice?"

Instead of replying, she toots angrily at an elderly lady who's taking a little too long to cross the zebra crossing.

"And you called him *Daddy*," Matty crows, bursting out laughing. "You're a grown-up!"

"Will you shut up?" she roars, causing all of us – even Layla – to flinch.

I lean forward to tap my little brother on the shoulder. "Just leave it, Matty."

He slumps into silence, but after a minute or so mutters, "Can I have one of your Oreos?"

"No, you bloody can't," Annalise growls, back in her normal voice.

"I will when we get home," he says boldly.

"You will not," she snaps. "They'll be kept in my case, which has a combination lock on, all right?"

Layla stares at me, eyes wide. *Mad*, she mouths at me. *I know*, I mouth back.

We drop Layla back at hers and although she says, "Thanks for taking us," as she gets out of the car, Annalise acts as if she doesn't hear. The atmosphere is so tense as she drives us home, it's as if all the fun we had at bowling never happened at all.

Next day, Mum is called into hospital for an emergency. I know Layla isn't around – she's persuaded her mum that her school skirt really is knicker-flashingly short, so they've driven to our nearest shopping mall. It's a cold, drizzly Sunday and Matty's so bored he's spent most of the morning swinging on the fridge door, trying to work out at which point the internal light comes on.

Our school clothes are ready, all ironed by Mum. I sit at the kitchen table, trying to get started on a history essay that we were meant to do over the holidays. Usually, Mum nags me to get any homework done at the start of the hols, but with everything that's happened, this kind of slipped through the net.

Annalise wanders into the kitchen, yawning and wearing a silky purple dressing gown and matching slippers. She's brought a smell with her too: Mum's favourite perfume. She *reeks* of it. I'd recognize it anywhere. "Er, what perfume are you wearing?" I ask, hoping it doesn't sound like I'm accusing her.

She shrugs. "Dunno. It was just lying around. . ."

On Mum's dressing table, she means. It's never anywhere else. What makes her think she can prowl around in Mum's room? She opens a cupboard and starts searching frantically among our packets and jars.

"What are you looking for?" Matty asks.

"Food," she replies.

"There's plenty to eat—" I start.

"I mean biscuits. Something decent to eat – not your bird-foody muesli or, or . . . *fruit.*" She glares at our piled-high fruit bowl as if it's full of poo.

"But you bought loads," I remind her, "while we were at the bowling alley. Didn't you say you were keeping them in your room?"

She shoots me a withering look. Why does she even want to be an au pair if young people annoy her so much? This is hardly the impression she gave when she was on the phone to *Daddy.* "They're all gone," she says.

"You ate all those already?" Matty blurts out. "You'll have no teeth!"

"Yes, thank you, Matty," she snaps. "What are you – a health inspector?" We both burst out laughing as she peers in the fridge and pulls out a packet of beansprouts. She mutters something I don't catch, then shoves them back in.

"You said the f-word!" Matty announces.

"No, I didn't. Just leave me alone."

He turns to me. "She did, Zoe. She said, *Effin' beansprouts*, I heard her. . . I'm gonna tell Mum!"

"Matty, c'mon – just forget it," I mutter.

"God, you two," she groans. "I'm not feeling well, all right? And I'm hungry and all you're doing is laughing at me." She sinks onto a kitchen chair looking pale and tired without her make-up.

I muster a sympathetic smile and sit beside her. "What's wrong?"

"Uhh . . . I dunno. Bit of a cold or something."

I inhale Mum's spicy perfume and decide it's best not to mention it. "Shall I make you some toast?" I ask.

Annalise shakes her head.

"I'll go out and get you something if you like," I add, thinking, I'll do *anything* to try and shift her black mood. Maybe she's homesick, and missing her own mum and dad.

A small smile warms her face. "Would you?"

"I'll go," Matty says quickly. "I like going to the shop. . ."

"Are you sure?" Annalise asks, turning to me. "Is it OK for him to go out by himself?"

"To the corner shop, yeah," I reply. "Matty – take some money from the jar and get Annalise a packet of biscuits—"

"All right." He grins, lifting down our jar of coins from the top of the fridge and stuffing a handful into his jeans pocket.

Annalise musters a proper smile. "That's kind of you, Matty. Thanks. Um . . . can you bring them up to my room, please? I'm feeling a bit shivery. Think I'll go back to bed."

"Sure," he says, already scampering towards the door.

Within minutes he's back, clutching an open packet of Oreos.

"Aren't those meant to be for Annalise?" I ask, frowning.

"I only had two." He sniggers and wipes a crumb from his mouth.

"Take the rest of them up to her then," I tell him. "Maybe that'll cheer her up."

He grins and hurries upstairs. Not like him to be so helpful, but maybe he's feeling guilty about laughing at her when she was feeling ill? Anyway, life will be easier for all of us if we can find a way to get along with Annalise, even if she does use Mum's lipstick and perfume and lie to her dad. Mum keeps saying "we need help", as if we were falling apart as a family before – which isn't true. I'd love it to be just the three of us again, though. Well, the *four* of us, if a miracle happened and Dad came back. But there's the baby now, so they'll be his family, not us. . .

I try to write more of my essay but it feels like my brain has shut down. Think. *Think*. I'm writing about the Industrial Revolution, and how children even younger than Matty were made to work long, long days in factories and were punished if they got tired. They were whipped and dunked into barrels of water and sometimes the girls had their hair cut off.

"What are *these*?" The roar from upstairs makes my pen jerk across my page. "What the hell *are* they?" Annalise yells. "Matty – come here!" I drop my pen and rush upstairs to find her on the landing, clutching a biscuit that's had a bite taken out of it. Matty's nowhere to be seen.

"Look at this," she exclaims, jabbing it in my face.

"Er, yes – it's an Oreo," I say.

"Don't try to be funny."

I squint at it in confusion. "It is," I insist. "Look – it's got the pattern stamped on. . ."

"I know what it is, Zoe," she snaps, which confuses me even more. What is this – a trick question?

"Why are you asking, then?" I jut out my chin to show I'm not scared.

She rolls her eyes. "Just try it."

"No, thanks," I say, stepping away from her.

"Go on, have a bite and tell me what you think."

"Why?" I'm standing up to her now, which makes me feel quite proud.

"Because it's not right. Someone's tampered with it. . ."

"What on earth are you talking about?" I take it from her outstretched hand. Although I'm not keen on eating a biscuit she's already bitten into, I give it the tiniest nibble.

"Ugh," I exclaim. "That's horrible. What's in it?"

"Don't ask me." She stomps to the bathroom, slurps water noisily from the tap and spits it out into the washbasin. From Matty's room comes a burst of hysterical laughter. Annalise's head shoots up from the sink. Barging past me on the landing, she pushes open Matty's bedroom door so hard, it slams against the wall.

"Hey," he cries out. "You'll scare Fanta."

"What?" she snaps at him.

He points at his fish, swimming lazily in its tank. "They don't like loud noises. They can die of shock, y'know."

"Never mind that," Annalise snarls. "What did you do to these biscuits?"

His cheeks redden, and now he's not looking quite so brave. He turns back to study his fish, tracing its movements with a finger on the glass.

"I said, *what did you do?*" she repeats.

"I took 'em apart and put toothpaste inside."

At that moment, Annalise looks as if she might actually explode. She opens her mouth and shuts it again, just like Fanta in his tank. "You *are* joking," she says slowly.

"No, I'm not," Matty says, all cheeky again. "I took a knife in my pocket and I bought the Oreos and a little tube of toothpaste. Then I took them apart and I scraped out the whiteish middles and squirted toothpaste on them instead. Then I sandwiched them back together."

There's a moment's stunned silence, then Annalise yells, "You horrible boy! D'you know I was nearly sick? I *hate* mint and I have a very sensitive stomach..."

"Why did you do that?" I hiss at him.

"'Cause she's horrible to us. She's grumpy and moany and she swears—"

"C'mon, Matty," I say, grabbing his hand and leading him downstairs. I know he can be the most irritating boy ever, but I don't want her shouting at him any more. In fact, it's a relief when she stays up in her room. Matty and I while away the rest of the day watching TV and messing about in the garden when the rain finally stops. I even agree to a game of hide-and-seek to keep him happy. And when Mum comes home, I decide it's best not to make a big deal of what happened today, because I don't want Matty to get into a whole heap of trouble. In fact, I only tell her because she keeps asking why we're so quiet.

"That was a horrid thing to do, Matty," she says over dinner. "Whatever made you play a trick like that?"

Matty jabs his fork into a heap of mashed potato. Luckily, Annalise reckoned she was "too ill" to come down and eat with us. "*She's* horrid," he blurts out. "She threw my breakfast in the bin!"

"What?" Mum frowns.

"And she's been using your perfume," I add. "She must've been in your room."

"Are you sure?"

"Yeah, I'm positive!"

She tuts and shakes her head. "I have to say, it sounds like you're both looking for things to pick fault with."

"Mum, that's not fair," I shoot back. "We're just trying to tell you what's been going on."

She rubs her tired eyes. "Well, I hope you'll both try and be more positive from now on. I really don't have the energy for all this."

I nod glumly.

"She swore as well," Matty adds.

Mum places her knife and fork neatly on her plate. "You mean Annalise swore at *you*?"

"No," he replies, "at the beansprouts."

"Oh, don't be ridiculous," she says, sounding really exasperated now.

"It's true," he insists. "She *hates* our food. . ."

With a huge sigh, Mum gets up from the table. "You two load the dishwasher, OK? I'm going up to have a little chat with her." As she leaves the kitchen, Matty and I exchange startled looks. Although we try to listen in, we can't make out what they're saying upstairs. Then there's laughter. They're actually *laughing* together, like old friends. This doesn't suggest that Mum's telling her off, or warning her that she'd better not insult our vegetables again.

Moments later, Mum reappears with a big smile. "What a fuss over nothing," she says, clicking on the kettle. "She thought the biscuit prank was quite funny actually." She chuckles again.

"But, Mum—" Matty protests.

She places her hands on his shoulders. "Listen, I can't have this, being hit with a whole list of complaints every time I come home from work. I need both of you to make a real effort from now on, OK? Honestly, I don't know what's got into you two."

Chapter twenty

Layla

Annalise stays out of our way now that Zoe's mum's not at work. "She says she's exhausted from taking us out all week," Zoe laughs as we lounge in her room, "and so am I. Anyway, Mum doesn't expect her to work at weekends."

"Thank God for that," I laugh, just grateful for the chance to hang out together. It's slightly odd, though. Annalise is free to do whatever she wants, but she seems to hang out in her room all the time.

"It feels like our house isn't ours any more," Zoe admits, and I know what she means: it's definitely changed around here. Zoe seems quiet too, as if something's on her mind. I want to talk about Ben, and what it'll be like seeing him at school on Monday, but don't want Zoe to think I'm obsessed. I've never held back my feelings like this before. So it's almost a relief when Monday morning rolls around, knowing he'll be there, just another boy at school, and things will start to feel normal again.

I love getting dressed when it's not for school. I can throw all kinds of colours together and know that no one else looks like me. But school uniform is different. White shirt, grey sweater, grey skirt and black blazer – even our shoes have to be plain black with "no embellishment", as they put it. It's like stepping into a black-and-white world.

Breakfast is bacon toasties, which should feel like a treat, but even the bacon turns out black today. Gran wandered off while Mum was in the middle of grilling it and so she asked me to keep an eye on it while she and Kyle went out to look for her – only I sort of forgot. It wasn't entirely my fault. I was too busy with Amber, who kept moaning, "My gym kit's still wet," and waving a pair of shorts in front of my face, as if I might be able to dry them with a magic stare.

Kyle and Mum are back now, with a confused-looking Gran, who says, "I just wanted to go to the shops. I thought I might buy myself a nice cardigan."

"The shops aren't open yet," Mum says, shaking her head.

"Ew, what happened to the bacon?" Kyle exclaims.

"I burned it," I mutter.

"Oh, Layla," Mum groans.

"And my gym kit's damp," Amber says, "*and* it's all smoky in here. . ." Agh, get me out of here, to the sanctuary of school. I say a quick goodbye, shrug on my jacket and head out without any breakfast. On my way, I text Zoe to say I'm early as I had to get out of the madhouse. She's waiting for me at our usual corner, outside Norelli's, looking super neat with her blonde hair tied back in a sleek ponytail. I haven't even managed to *brush* mine, and there's a bacony whiff hanging around me like a cloud.

"Honestly," she says, laughing, when I tell her the story, "you don't smell of anything."

"Are you sure?"

"Yeah," she says, nudging me as CJ appears across the street with Sadie, Kim and Anja. They're her devoted followers and tend to move in a pack. Right now, they are cackling wildly and don't seem to have noticed us.

"My clothes are too big as well," I hiss at Zoe. "I've got a belt on to hold this skirt up, and look how baggy and shapeless this jumper is."

"There's nothing wrong with it," she reassures me.

I kick a polystyrene takeaway carton out of our way. "Mum insisted on buying a bigger size. Said it's best to have some growing room – the way you do when you're seven years old. . ."

Zoe glances at me. "You look fine. Stop worrying. Anyway, what d'you think everyone at school'll make of Ben?"

What can I say? "He's going to be so popular, he

won't even glance in our direction," I reply with a shrug.

She smiles at me. "He's got your number, though. . ."

"That doesn't mean anything."

"Yes, it does," she says firmly.

I force a smile, sensing my face is boiling up. She's going to notice and want to discuss him some more, which'll make it even worse. I *never* felt awkward around Zoe before Ben moved here. Sometimes I wish things were the way they used to be, before the Easter holidays, or even further back when boys were just boys – sometimes annoying, sometimes nice, but not so different from us.

"Hey – Layla!" CJ's voice rings out across the street.

"Ignore her," Zoe mutters as we walk on.

"*Layla!*" CJ shouts again.

"I wish she'd stop yelling," I hiss at Zoe.

"Yeah, let's hurry up. . ." As we quicken our pace, CJ breaks away from the others and tears across the street towards us. I glance at Zoe, sensing her fear that all that cow-face stuff might blow up again. I know she's been hoping that everyone's forgotten about it during the holidays.

"Wait," CJ calls out, scampering towards us.

We both stop and look at her. "What is it?" I ask.

Pink blotches have formed on her cheeks. "D'you know anything about that poster?" She points across the street, where her friends have gathered around a noticeboard. No one ever puts up anything interesting, unless you're keen on flower-arranging classes or church outings.

"What poster?" Zoe asks with a frown.

"Come and look." She smiles expectantly, and for a moment, I wonder whether there's another – nicer – CJ underneath.

"All right," I say cautiously. We cross the road and peer at the noticeboard. The usual posters about toddler clubs and Sunday school events all fade away because there, in the middle, is Ben's face, staring out at us.

"Oh!" Zoe exclaims.

"You know him, don't you?" CJ says, turning back to gaze at the poster.

"A bit," I say with a shrug.

"He hangs out with your brother, doesn't he?"

"Sometimes," I say, giving Zoe a quick look.

Kim starts giggling. "Can you introduce us?"

Sadie snorts into her hand. "Bet they want to keep him all to themselves."

"Don't be stupid," Zoe retorts.

"Oh," Anja crows to the others, "I forgot that Zoe thinks she's better than us 'cause her mum's been on TV. . ."

"Shut up," I snap, seeing my best friend's face fall. All this, and we're not even at school yet. I'm filled with an urge to say, *Come on, let's grab our bikes and cycle far away, to Dean House, and hang out in the tree house all day. . .* Instead, I cut CJ and the others out of my vision and read the poster:

Save the Acorn!

Fund-raising concert featuring singer-songwriter

Ben Rawlings*

(*Yeah, in massive type like that. Underneath there's a black-and-white photo of him — *just Ben by himself* — looking wistful and gorgeous with his hair mussed up, strumming an acoustic guitar.) I look at Zoe. She looks at me. Beneath the photo it says:

Saturday 4th May, 7.30 p.m. at the Acorn Theatre
Adults £5, Children £3
Plus!!! Want to be a guest singer on the night?
Auditions for vocalists will be held at 2 p.m.
on Saturday 20th April in the garage
at 17 Hunter Crescent.
All welcome!

Danny and Jude's place. Wonder how Jude feels about that? "Why's it just Ben in the photo?" Zoe blurts out.

"I don't know. I thought the others were playing—"

"Who cares about the others?" CJ sniggers. "I've seen him around. He was at the vintage market, wasn't he? The day we—"

"Yeah, OK," I snap, not wanting to be reminded of the most humiliating day in my life to date.

"Well," she goes on, smirking at her friends, "all I can say is, no wonder it's just him on the poster and not the others."

"What's wrong with the others?" Zoe asks sharply.

CJ bursts out laughing. "That bunch of losers? Who'd want to watch *them*?"

I'm furious now, and I can tell Zoe is too. That's my brother she's talking about.

"This isn't what Ben had in mind," I mutter to Zoe. "He said the band would play. Ben, Kyle and Danny—"

"And Jude," Zoe adds, grabbing my arm and forcing me to walk away.

"No, he left the band, remember?"

"No wonder," CJ sniggers behind us. "He's *embarrassing. . .*"

I spin around to face her. "No, he's not. He's a brilliant guitarist *and* he has a great voice. What would you know, anyway? You've never heard him play—"

"He's a nerd," she snorts, "who hangs around with his big brother 'cause he hasn't got any mates of his own."

I glare at her, wondering how I could have thought, for even a brief moment, that she's actually OK. "C'mon," I say, nudging Zoe. "We're going to be late." We start walking faster, my too-big skirt swishing around my legs. And although I'm trying not to listen, little fragments of conversation ping into my ears:

Kim: Are you going to the auditions, CJ?

CJ, pretending she couldn't possibly: Ooh, no. I'd never sing in front of an audience. I'm far too shy.

Sadie: You should, you know. Your voice is amazing. More people should hear it.

CJ: I'd just die!

Anja: Honestly, people would pay just to see you! You're bound to get picked. How many is he gonna choose, d'you think?

All goes silent behind us. "Ugh, I'm glad we've got nothing to do with this," I whisper to Zoe.

"Me too."

Then from behind us, CJ blasts out, "Bet those two losers are going to do it 'cause they were in that pathetic junior choir..." Zoe and I look at each other in horror as they all burst into song – something we learned at choir when we were about eleven. We had to perform it in front of a packed theatre and I was so proud, especially as Zoe and I were asked to sing one verse all by ourselves, as a duet. Mum, Dad, Gran and Kyle came to see us (Amber too, although she just played with her Beanie Babies on the floor). Zoe's mum and dad were still together then, and sat next to my family on the front row. It went so well we were asked to perform the duet again at school.

And now, CJ and her tribe are wailing moronically behind us... "They think they're the best singers in school," she cackles. "Remember that duet they did last

Christmas? It's always the two of them, stuck together, killing our ears!" There's a gale of rowdy laughter.

"For God's sake," Zoe mutters.

"They're so stupid" I mutter, my cheeks burning as we walk even faster to get away from them. Gradually, the snide voices fade. Zoe tries to cheer me up by describing Matty's prank with the Oreos, and I tell her that Amber's salmon purse is still festering away in its plastic box in our yard, and that no one's allowed to throw it away because it's "art".

"Imagine what'll happen," Zoe says, "when someone finally takes the lid off." We giggle over this, but both of us are faking it really as it's hardly been the best start to the day.

"Look!" Zoe exclaims as we approach the school gates.

At first I don't know what she's talking about. "Look," she hisses again, "it's him!"

Ben, she means, a little way ahead of us. "He seems a bit lost," I suggest as he wanders into the grounds, that burgundy rucksack he had on the day we met in the tree house now slung low on his back.

"Let's say hi," she says.

I swallow hard. "Are you sure?"

"Yeah," she says. "Why not?" So we hurry ahead, leaving CJ and the others behind us as we catch up with Ben.

"Hey," he says, grinning.

"Hey." I smile, adding, "First day, huh?" It's all I can think of to say.

"Yeah." Although he sounds relaxed and confident, there's a flicker of something else in his eyes. Like he's not quite as at home here as he'd like to be. At least, not yet.

"Kyle'll be here soon – he normally cuts it a bit fine," I add. "I'm sure he'll help you find your way round."

"Great," Ben says as the three of us head towards the main entrance.

"D'you know where you're supposed to go?" Zoe asks.

"Er . . . the office, I guess?"

I smile. "They *are* expecting you, aren't they?"

"Yeah, of course. . ."

"Which teachers did you meet when you were shown round?"

He doesn't reply for a moment. "I, um . . . I wasn't really."

Zoe squints at him as we push open the glass doors and go inside. "D'you mean you haven't actually been here before?"

"Er, nope."

"Didn't your parents look around," I ask, "to check it's OK?" *To make sure it's up to boarding-school standards*, is what I mean.

"They didn't have time," Ben says quickly.

"Oh." I force another big smile. "Well, that's the office over there. . ."

"Thanks," he says, making his way to the glass partition that separates Mrs Owen, one of the office ladies, from us pupils. Zoe and I hang back and watch. Ben has already attracted admiring looks from a few girls, although he doesn't seem aware of it. He's too busy explaining who he is to Mrs Owen, who nods and gives him a warm smile. I can't help noticing him glancing around, as if wondering how he's going to fit in.

There's no chance to talk to Ben at break, or even at lunchtime. Whenever Zoe and I spot him, there's a cluster of people fluttering around him, like fish all homing in on the same flake of food.

"Told you he'd be popular," I say as Zoe and I eat our pizza slices in the canteen.

She nods and takes a big bite. "You were right."

I take a bite too, and then spot Jude heading away from the serving area. I beckon him over. His face brightens as he carries his tray towards us.

"OK if I sit with you?" he asks.

"Sure," I say, and he takes the seat next to mine.

"Have you seen the posters for the Acorn concert?" Zoe asks.

His smile slips a bit. "Er, yeah."

"I don't get what's going on with the band," I say, without thinking. "Why is it just Ben on the poster, with no mention of anyone else?"

I feel bad even mentioning it, but he shrugs and says, "Maybe they all agreed that'd be best?"

"Why, though?" Zoe asks.

Jude looks at his baguette. "No idea. I'm glad to be out of it, to be honest. . ." I stare at him, wondering how he's managing to handle it so well. After all, Ben marched right in and took his place. "It's different now," he adds, "but maybe that's a good thing. I mean, we've been playing for years and never really got anywhere. We haven't played a single gig. We don't even have a name, for God's sake. And now Ben's come along, the guys have got a gig right away."

I glance across the dining room. Ben is installed at a table surrounded by CJ, Sadie, Anja and Kim. I notice Kyle, Danny and Harris are with them but they don't look happy about it. Jude's right: everything *is* different. Maybe not in a good way, though.

The afternoon passes in a haze of gossip – virtually every girl in our year is desperate to know about Ben – and at home time, I happen to glance at the noticeboard beside the office. All the usual stuff is there: the latest school newsletter and stuff about netball tournaments, chess club and teachers doing a sponsored cycle ride.

And there, right in the middle – partly covering some of the other stuff – is the Acorn fund-raiser poster with Ben's face beaming out. Around it, in bright red felt-tip, someone has drawn a huge heart.

Chapter twenty-one

Zoe

By the end of the day, Ben's face is all over town. Apart from at school, and on the main noticeboard in the middle of town, posters have appeared in tons of shop windows. Everywhere I look, he's there. Even Annalise has seen them. "You going to these auditions on Saturday?" she asks next morning, applying her make-up while I make toast for Matty and me.

I take a slurp of orange juice. "I don't think so," I reply.

She peers at me across the table, her lipstick – no, it's *Mum's* lipstick – hovering close to her mouth. She must have taken it from her room after she left early for work this morning. "I am," she announces.

By some miracle, I manage to keep a straight face. "Can you sing?" I ask.

"Yeah, course I can."

I blink at her, hardly able to swallow my toast. "You mean, you want to be one of the guest singers?"

"Why not? I've got to do *something*. It's so boring around here, I think I'm going mad."

I throw her a look that says, *You're already there*. I'm pretty sure that Matty, who seems to have frozen with his spoon half way to his mouth, is thinking the same.

"You can't sing at the concert," he declares.

"Why not?" Annalise's nostrils flare open, as if a big gust of air has puffed them out.

"'Cause you're too old!"

"No, I'm not," she retorts, jamming the lid back on the lipstick without winding it down properly. "Oh – look what you've made me do," she gasps, pulling the lid off again. "I've squashed it." Hmm, Mum'll be *delighted* about that.

"You can't sing at the Acorn," Matty says firmly.

"Yes, I can! What d'you mean, I'm too old? I'm only eighteen." I stare at her across the table, then hand Matty his rucksack and grab my own bag from the hall. Annalise is supposed to take Matty to school, but she's showing no sign of getting ready to leave.

"Shall I take him, then?" I ask.

She frowns slightly. "I'll do it if you want. What time does school start again?"

And she's meant to love working with children?

"Never mind," I mutter as my brother and I step out into the bright spring day.

After dropping Matty off, I hurry on to meet Layla at our corner.

"Annalise wants to audition for the concert," I blurt out.

"You're kidding! She doesn't even know anyone."

I shrug. "It did say 'all welcome' on the poster. God, it'll be so embarrassing when everyone finds out she lives with us! What can I do?"

"Nothing, I guess," Layla says glumly. "This is gonna be a disaster, I can tell."

In fact, everyone else seems to think it's the best idea ever. CJ, Sadie, Kim and Anja, plus virtually every other girl in our year, is planning to audition. No boys so far. Most of them wouldn't be seen dead singing onstage – apart from Jude, and of course, he's having nothing to do with this.

"You know what?" Layla says as we wander home after school. "I think we should do it."

"You mean the auditions?" I gawp at her.

"Yeah. Oh, come on. We've been singing together all our lives, haven't we? If everyone else is taking part – if *Annalise* is doing it – then why don't we?"

I hesitate, not wanting to sound pathetic. But the truth is, I'm not so sure about singing in front of Ben. I *never* felt self-conscious onstage before he showed up but now... "OK," I say carefully. "But only if you promise we can sing together."

She envelopes me in a hug. "Of course! Promise. You know I'd never do it without you."

After we've said bye at the corner, I'm so preoccupied that I barely notice the bike whizzing by. It's raining, and I just want to cosy up at home. The bike stops ahead, and Ben turns around. "Want a lift?" he asks with a grin.

"No, thanks," I laugh. "I didn't know you cycled to school. . ."

He nods. No helmet, I notice. "Yeah."

"Even in the rain? Doesn't someone pick you up?"

"Nah, it's OK," he says quickly. "So, are you coming on Saturday?"

"To the auditions? Yes – me and Layla are going to sing together."

He climbs off his bike and wheels it over. "Together? Why don't you sing by yourself?"

"Um, I never have," I explain. "Sung solo, I mean."

"You should," he exclaims. "Your voice is really good. I heard that secret recording Kyle made of the two of you . . ."

"That was awful!" I exclaim, blushing madly.

"No, it wasn't. . ." He gives me a look that makes my heart somersault.

Does he *really* like my voice, or is he just trying to flatter me?

"Sometimes," he adds, "it's good to stand up there all on your own."

"I don't think I'm brave enough," I say with a small laugh.

His eyes meet mine, and it feels as if everything – cars, people hurrying home from the shops and school – all fade to nothing. "You can be anything you want to be," he says with a smile.

I shrug. "I don't know about that."

He touches my arm. "C'mon, Zoe. You're so pretty you should be up there in the spotlight all by yourself."

Before I can even utter a word, he's back on his bike and cycling away into the grey, rainy afternoon. No one's *ever* said I'm pretty before. Well, Mum has, and Layla, of course. But not a boy. No one like Ben. But then, I've never, ever met anyone like him before.

I watch him, my heart dancing for joy until he turns the corner, out of sight.

Layla and I practise all week. Every spare minute we have, we're either up in Layla's room, having bribed Amber with sweets to stay out of our way, or at my place with my bedroom door firmly shut. I don't tell Layla what Ben said on Tuesday because it would sound like the most big-headed thing ever. He was probably only trying to boost my confidence for the auditions. Instead, I try to push him out of my mind and focus on singing. And I try not to think about what it would be like if, instead of us performing together, it was just me on my own, in the spotlight, like Ben said.

On Saturday morning, the day of the auditions,

we stand on my balcony and sing over the garden, pretending there's an audience down there. We've picked one of the songs we sang in the choir – our leader, Mr Duffy, wrote it especially for us. It's a simple melody that splits into harmonies and seems to suit our voices perfectly.

"Well done!" Mum cries up from the lawn.

"I didn't know you were out there," I exclaim.

She smiles. It's not one of those quick, tense smiles that she flashes when she's about to rush off to work, or the tired one she musters when she comes home. It's a big, beaming smile that says she's proud of us. I look at Layla, who grins at me, and right then I know everything's going to be all right.

"We *can* do it," I say as we step back inside.

"Course we can," she laughs.

"Wish we could head over to the auditions together . . . we could get some last-minute practice in on the way."

"I know," Layla says, "but Mum wants me to go home first 'cause Aunty Claire's coming for lunch. It'll be easier to just meet you there."

"You will be able to get away, though, won't you?"

"Yeah, of course – I've just got to be around to say hi. God, I don't think I'll be able to eat a thing. . . Hey," she giggles, "you'll be OK – you can go with Annalise. . ."

"Thanks a lot," I wail. It's only a ten-minute walk

over to Danny and Jude's place, where the auditions are taking place, but I don't want to be stuck with her any longer than necessary.

"I'd better go now," Layla adds.

We hug and dissolve into fits of laughter on our doorstep, a mixture of excitement and nerves.

Annalise is nowhere to be seen, which is a relief. I don't fancy getting into a discussion about the auditions with her.

"Are you excited?" Mum asks, setting out lunch for Matty and me. "I know you're going to be brilliant."

"Thanks, Mum. And, yeah, I s'pose I am. But nervous, though."

"Annalise is going to audition too," Matty adds with a snort.

"Is she?" Mum's eyes widen. "Well, that's good, isn't it? She's joining in with local things. . ."

I fetch cutlery from the drawer and set the table. "S'pose so," I say, trying to sound as if I'm at least making an effort to like her. I haven't even told Mum about Annalise squashing her lipstick or using her favourite perfume. Got to be *positive*, right?

"Very brave of her, I'd say," Mum adds. "Considering she's new around here."

"So's Ben," I blurt out, immediately wishing I hadn't.

"Ah," Mum says with a teasing grin, "I've heard a lot about this mysterious Ben."

"Have you?" I say, foraging about in the fridge, just

for something to do. I pull out a jar of pickled gherkins, even though I can't stand them.

"I could hardly miss him," Mum says, "with all those posters pinned up around town. And I ran into Layla's mum the other day – she said he's constantly round at their house, practising for this concert."

I plonk the gherkin jar on the table. Mum gives it a bemused look as if it might be poised to do a trick.

"Yeah, um, he's actually organized the whole thing," I mutter.

Mum smiles approvingly. "Isn't it great, someone arriving in a quiet little place like this, determined to make things happen?"

I nod, wanting to get lunch over and done with so I can hide away in my room and have a last run-through of my part of our song. And it *is* our song: mine and Layla's. No one else will sing anything like it. Hopefully, it'll make us stand out. Either that, or everyone'll fall about laughing because it's not exactly a chart-type thing. . .

I swallow hard. "Where is Annalise, anyway?"

"She went to the hairdresser's," Mum replies.

"What for?"

Mum chuckles. "To have her hair cut, I'd imagine. Or coloured. Both, probably – she went a couple of hours ago." God, she's probably having something *amazing* done, especially for the auditions. Maybe that's what's needed for an occasion like this? I can't even apply eyeliner without looking like a panda, apparently. I glance down at my blue-and-white striped T-shirt, jeans and flat sandals, and picture Annalise, in her short skirt and heels, grabbing the microphone and belting out a song. What if she really *can* sing and outshines us all?

"Mum," I say quietly, "d'you think I look OK?"

She turns to me and smiles. "You look lovely, darling. You always do. You're very lucky to be naturally pretty."

I try to smile back, and to replay what Ben said on Tuesday – something about me being in the spotlight? Do I *want* that, though? I've always hidden in the shadows, really. Layla's the one who stands out, with her amazing clothes and sunny confidence.

After lunch – which I can only pick at – I grab my jacket and give Mum a hug. "Good luck, sweetheart," she says, holding me close.

"I'm coming too!" Matty yelps.

We both swing round to see him already pulling on his trainers. "Oh, Matty, no," I groan.

"Please!" he begs. "I won't get in the way, I promise."

Mum grimaces. "He's desperate to watch you," she murmurs. "He's been on and on at me all morning."

"But, Mum—"

"C'mon," he says, grinning. "I'll be your – what do you call it, that thing people have at football matches?"

I glance back at Mum, who's giving me such an encouraging smile, like she *really* believes in me, that I don't have the heart to say no.

"A mascot," I mutter.

"I'll be your mascot," he says, charging for the door. "I'm gonna make you lucky today."

Chapter twenty-two

Layla

"Layla? LAYLA?"

"Coming, Mum," I call back, giving myself a final check in the mirror and deciding my denim shorts are fine, and my bright blue top is fine, as are the purple-and-black stripy tights and the black DMs that I found in the charity shop the other day, hardly scuffed and just my size. Yeah, everything's *fine*. We've had lunch, and I've chatted to Auntie Claire, and now I just want to get going.

I clatter downstairs to be greeted by Amber. "Gran's missing!" she announces, her eyes round with worry.

"What? Where's she gone?"

"We don't know," she cries. I turn to see Mum and Aunty Claire in the kitchen doorway, looking worried.

"Have you any idea where she might be?" Mum asks. "Claire and I were just washing up, and when I popped back into the living room, she'd gone."

197

"We've looked everywhere," Aunty Claire adds. "All over the house and out in the street . . ."

"I don't know where else she'd be," I say. "What d'you think we should do?"

Aunty Claire shakes her head. "I've said it before: you should keep the front door locked."

"It's her home," Mum mutters. "Not a prison—"

"But look what's happened!" Aunty Claire exclaims.

Mum sighs loudly. Aunty Claire – Mum's sister – is lovely, but sometimes she's a bit too bossy for Mum's liking. "I don't know *what* to do," Mum tells me. "I've called Dad and he's coming straight back to help us look for her." She checks her watch. "He'll be here any minute. Kyle's already left for the auditions. . ."

"I'll check the yard," I say quickly, hurrying out in case Gran's got mixed up and is having her morning cigarette at at twenty to two in the afternoon. Nothing – just her plastic chair and Amber's fish purse sitting beneath it in its box.

"Dad's here," Mum says as I go back inside. "Let's all start looking. . ."

"But the auditions!" As soon as the words have popped out of my mouth, I'd give anything to stuff them back in again. "What about them?" Mum snaps.

"You care more about the auditions than Gran!" Amber announces.

"Of course I don't," I exclaim. "It's just—"

"Kevin," Mum interrupts, turning to Dad, "you

take Amber and drive around and look for her. Me, Claire and Layla will go on foot, all right? That way, we'll be covering the roads and all the footpaths and the park. . . And, Layla, you might be a little bit late, but that doesn't matter, does it? You can text Zoe and explain."

They're all looking at me. I swallow and nod. "Of course, Mum."

"Good," Dad says firmly, taking Amber by the hand and leading her outside to his taxi.

I blink at Mum, feeling like the most selfish person on earth. "Sorry, Mum," I murmur. "And don't worry, we'll find Gran."

"I hope so." She tries to muster a smile, but instead of her mouth turning up at the corners, it stays pretty much dead straight. "C'mon, sweetheart, let's go."

And so we set off, heading for Norelli's first to ask if anyone's seen Gran walking past. No luck there. The three of us make for the park, where there's only an old lady with her dog. She hasn't seen Gran wandering about, either. "Could you keep a lookout for her?" Mum asks, looking really stressed now. "She's wearing a pink flowery dress and, er, a sort of rusty-coloured cardie, I think. . ."

"Of course I will," the lady says kindly.

"*Someone* will have seen her," Aunty Claire tries to reassure Mum.

Next we make for my school and check all the

grounds, including behind the canteen where CJ and her pack like to hang out, and the garden we planted last year.

"I'll try Kyle," Mum says. "Maybe he could have a look around the streets near Jude and Danny's house." She puts her phone to her ear, sighing loudly, then stuffs it back into her jeans pocket. "Does that boy *ever* answer his phone? What's the point in him having it if he never bloody switches it on?"

It's so unlike her to snap like that. "They've probably started playing," I say, squeezing her hand. "He won't hear it above his drums."

I think of them all in the garage at Danny and Jude's. I imagine Zoe making her way there right now, all excited. Maybe she's even arrived and is wondering where I am. I wish I could let her know what's happened, but in all the panic I realize I've left my phone at home. Still, Zoe will understand if I'm a bit late. Right now, all I want is for Gran to be safely back home.

Chapter twenty-three

Zoe

All the way there, Matty chatters on. Morbid stuff, mainly, about how long I think Fanta's going to live. Mum's warned him that fairground fish don't tend to survive long, but he read about one that's sixteen years old and is still alive now. I'm only half listening as my head is full of other stuff, like: I'm about to walk into Danny and Jude's garage with everyone there. Like Ben. With my little brother hanging about, rattling on about his fish. And me and Layla will sing, and Ben will decide whether we're good enough. It's bound to be him who makes the decision. He seems to decide everything around here. Like having just *his* name and *his* photo on the poster. The kind of person who makes things happen, Mum said. Well, she was right about that.

We're outside Danny and Jude's house now and I can already hear Kyle playing the drums. He doesn't make a big thing about it, but it sounds effortless, the way he plays. The main garage door is shut. I pause at the side door with Matty tugging at my arm, saying, "Zoe? Are we going in or not?"

"In a minute," I say, conscious of my heart beating way faster than normal. As fast as Kyle's drumbeat in fact. *Bang-bang-bang*, like it's about to burst out of my chest. *Ben's* in there. I'd give anything to turn on my heels and run – but I can't let Layla down. She's probably in there already. That thought makes me feel slightly better as I push open the door and walk in.

It's only just gone two o'clock and the garage is already milling with people. There's Ben, who's too busy tuning his guitar to pay attention to anyone, and Danny . . . and Jude, which is a surprise – I'd imagined he'd be steering clear, seeing as he's left the band. No Layla, though. I clear my throat, wondering where to stand and what to do with myself, which is stupid really as I know every single person here.

There's CJ, with her friends, all cackling away in the corner. Boxes of tools and stacks of plant pots are piled up on both sides, and Kyle's drum kit has been set up. When he spots me, his face breaks into a grin, which makes my nervousness fade a little. I'll feel better when Layla's here. Surely she'll be here any minute. Everyone's chatting away, not looking remotely scared. "I sing all the time," CJ is boasting to Kyle.

"Yeah?" he sniggers. "Like, where?"

"In the shower," she retorts.

"Wait till you hear her," Anja exclaims. She paws at CJ's arm in adoration. "They're gonna *die* when you start singing. . ."

"Die of pain, probably," Jude mutters by my side. I smile, trying to look relaxed, like this is no big deal at all.

"Didn't expect you to be here today," I say.

"Yeah, well, there's no hard feelings." He glances towards the door. "Isn't Layla coming?"

I nod. "She's supposed to be. Not sure what's happened to her." His gaze flickers towards the door again, and when he realizes I'm watching, he blushes and hurries away to perch on a scruffy old workbench.

Ben starts to strum his guitar and hum a melody. *Still* no sign of Layla. Would it really be so awful to grab Matty by the hand and creep away? I glance over to where he's tapping away at Kyle's cymbals. Amazingly, Kyle doesn't seem to mind.

We could leave. I could call him over, whisper that I'll buy him sweets, and no one would notice or care.

The door flies open. A tall, skinny girl with flaming red hair has marched in, wearing a tight red T-shirt, tiny denim hot pants and huge platform sandals with cork soles that clip-clop as she walks. "Annalise!" I gasp.

"What happened to your hair?" Matty yells.

She casts us a quick, irritated glance and scans the garage for someone important enough to talk to. Everyone's fallen silent. Danny's mouth has dropped open in shock. "When do the auditions start?" she asks.

"Er, pretty soon," Kyle says, looking flustered. I'm transfixed by her hair: dyed bright tangerine and piled up on top of her head, so stiff it looks like it'd crack if you tapped it. She gives Kyle a chilly smile, then makes straight for Ben.

"You're the one who's organizing this," she announces. "I've seen your picture everywhere."

"Er, yeah." He looks up at the creature towering above him.

"Can I sing then?" Annalise asks, like we've all been waiting for her to arrive.

"Of course you can." His mouth is suspiciously straight, and I wonder if he's trying not to laugh.

"So where's the mic?" She looks around, and I pull out my phone and call Layla, ready to tell her to get here *right now* – she won't want to miss this. But it just goes to voicemail, and no one picks up her house phone, either.

"Can you wait just a minute?" Danny asks, plugging cables into the amp. I try to look straight ahead but my eyes keep drifting back to the door, hoping Layla's about to step through. Jessie Hanley, who sang a solo at our last school concert, has arrived, along with Abby North, who all the boys like, though she's too cool to even bother with them. Annalise glances at me and scowls. More girls wander in, chatting excitedly and sneaking glances at Ben.

"OK, everyone." Ben has put his guitar in its stand

and is addressing the crowd, as if he does this kind of thing all the time. "If you want to audition, come up and give your name to Kyle, OK?"

"How many singers are you choosing?" Annalise calls out.

Ben raises a brow. "This isn't one of those awful talent contests. As long as you're confident and can hold a tune, then you can sing at the concert."

As long as you're confident, like that's no big deal. My insides are swirling like a washing machine now, and even though Kyle keeps giving me *it'll-be-OK* glances, it's hard to believe that it will. I shuffle up to Ben and he writes down my name on his list.

"Right," Ben calls out, "we're ready." Everyone falls silent. "Jessie first, please," he says, and she strides confidently towards the mic. Her long, straight golden hair is actually shining, as if illuminated from the inside.

CJ leans back against a rusty lawnmower, trying to look cool. I'm wondering now if she's really here to audition seriously, or just wants to shake things up. I check the door again . . . still no Layla, although a few more girls from school have drifted into the garage.

Layla's now almost half an hour late. I glance around the garage, at all the girls, and realize they're all staring at Ben. It doesn't look like any boys are going to audition today. It's just girls, girls, girls – all desperate to impress him, to be the one. . .

Across the garage, Kyle flashes a wide, wide grin.

Jessie starts to sing. She's picked a ballad, and her voice carries it brilliantly, with only the odd wobbly note when it goes a bit too high for her.

"Pretty good, isn't she?" I jump and realize that Ben's right next to me.

"Yeah," I whisper back.

"You will be too." He smiles encouragingly, holding my gaze for just a beat too long. Is he flirting, or is this the way he always acts around girls? "Er, is it OK if I have your number?" he asks.

For a moment, I'm stunned. "Sure," I mumble, taking his phone from him to type it in. I feel dazed. Normally I'd be thrilled by the attention, but right now it feels a bit too much. And he asked for Layla's number too. What's going on? I edge away as Jessie finishes her song to enthusiastic applause.

"That was fantastic," I say as she glides past me.

"Thanks!" She smiles broadly as Abby steps up to the mic. She's not as confident – you can hear the nerves in her voice – but she keeps catching Ben's eye, and he smiles encouragingly and gradually her courage builds. Everyone claps as, looking relieved that it's over, she hurries back to Jessie.

More girls sing. No one is awful, even the ones who start off with trembling hands, or keep licking their dry lips, or put their mouths too close to the mic so it makes a big *pfff* noise. There's a burst of applause after each performance, until Ben steps forward and says, "OK, one last song. . ." And for a horrible moment I think he means the last of the day, and that he doesn't want me to sing at all, which might be a blessing after all. But he carries on: "Then we'll take a break from the auditions and I'll play a couple of my songs before we finish with the final try-outs. So don't worry – everyone who wants to sing will get the chance today."

Out of the corner of my eye, I catch Kyle's eye again as he chats to Jude. Like me, Jude keeps checking the door. Where *is* Layla? I call both her mobile and landline again – no answer – and by the time I've shoved my phone back into my pocket, Annalise is standing in the middle of the garage, clutching the microphone.

Her first note is so loud, someone actually gasps. I've never heard anything like it. She is swaying and throwing her head back dramatically as she blasts out a song I don't recognize. It swoops down too low for her voice, then screeches so high I can actually see people wincing, including Ben – although Annalise doesn't notice as her eyes are screwed up tight. She finishes with a flourish.

"Wow," Ben says, taking the mic from her. "Thanks, er. . ."

"Annalise," she says with a big, scary grin.

"Right."

"So, am I in the concert or not?"

He looks around nervously. "Er, we're deciding all that at the end – once everyone's performed."

"Can I go next?" CJ calls out.

"After the break," Ben says, pulling his guitar strap over his head and murmuring something to Kyle and Danny. They launch into a song too quickly, and Kyle misses the first beat – but they get it together as Ben's voice rings out. He sounds great, and the song is incredibly catchy, like something you'd hear on the radio. I daren't look at Jude. There's a cheer as the song ends, then they launch straight into another, which has everyone clapping like mad. Poor Jude. They never did anything like this when he was in the band.

They've barely finished when CJ stomps towards Ben and says, "Is it time for more auditions now?" She rakes back her roughly chopped fair hair and smiles flirtatiously.

"OK," he says, laughing, actually looking impressed by her determination.

"Right." She grabs the mic, and a strange thing happens. Her face, which is usually so brittle and mean, seems to soften. Her eyes shine and a respectful hush falls over the garage. She opens her mouth.

And she's *amazing*. Every single person is transfixed. She's better than Jessie – better, even, than Ben. I've stopped glancing round for Layla at the garage door, and everyone seems to have forgotten about Annalise, who's sulking in a dark corner. I spot Matty, leaning against an old barrel next to Jude, and even he looks mesmerized.

Then a thought hits me: I can't sing now. It's not just that Layla hasn't turned up. It's because whatever I do will sound terrible compared to CJ's incredible voice.

All that rehearsing, for nothing.

"Zoe?" With a start, I realize everyone's staring at me. "Zoe," Ben says, "you do still want to sing, don't you?"

No! Of course I don't. I'd rather slice off my own hand with those rusty old garden shears sitting on the shelf. . .

"C'mon, Zo," Matty yells, turning to Kyle with a grin. "My sister's a *great* singer."

"Yeah, I know she is," Kyle says, throwing me an encouraging smile.

I clear my throat, still rooted to the spot. "I'd, er, rather wait till Layla shows up. We're doing it together," I add, realizing how lame that sounds, after every other girl has sung by herself.

Ben turns to Kyle. "D'you know where she is?"

Kyle frowns and shakes his head.

"Sorry," Ben says, "but we need to get going. She's already over an hour late. . ."

I nod miserably.

"Yeah, and we want to find out who's been chosen," snaps Annalise, just as her mobile rings in her pocket. "Daddy?" she says, flushing red as she answers it. "Erm, can I call you back? I'm just out with the children. . . Yes, Daddy, everything's fine." That weird posh voice again. She jams her phone back in her pocket and fixes on a determined glare.

"Look," Ben says, turning towards her, "I'm really sorry but I think I should tell you now – we don't think your, er, vocal style quite fits with what we're trying to do."

"What d'you mean?" she snaps. "It's just a stupid little concert, isn't it?"

She scans the room and it suddenly seems to dawn on her. "Am I the only one who's not gonna be chosen?" she blasts out.

"Yeah," Matty sniggers. "You're rubbish, Annalise!"

She swings round to face him, cheeks blazing with fury. "What are you doing here anyway? This has got nothing to do with you—"

"It's nothing to do with you, either," he snaps back. "You can't sing. Everyone was laughing—"

"No, they weren't—"

"Zoe, please," Ben cuts in, desperate for a distraction. "Come on – you can do it. And, you two –" he indicates Annalise and Matty, who are standing inches apart now, beaming hatred at each other "– this isn't what today's all about. The concert's meant to be a *good* thing, to save the theatre and involve everyone—"

"Yeah," Annalise yells, "everyone but *me*." She turns on her clompy platforms and marches out of the garage, slamming the door so hard behind her it causes Kyle's cymbal to make a shimmery sound.

For a moment, no one speaks. "Zoe," Kyle calls out, "you ready to sing now?"

I nod and step towards him. There's a flicker of something between us, as if he realizes how much I want Layla to be here but has complete confidence I can do it on my own.

Good luck, he mouths with a wink.

I smile, my heart beating a little faster. "Thanks," I whisper back.

Ben is looking at me. Everyone is. I'm no longer scared, but filled with courage I never knew I had. As I open my mouth, my phone trills into life. How could I have forgotten to turn it off? I let out a gasp and someone sniggers as I answer the call.

"Zoe, is Kyle with you?" It's Layla's mum, and she sounds frantic.

"Er, yes, he's right here—"

"Can I speak to him, please. It's Gran – she's missing and I'm so worried. . ."

I walk away from the microphone, hand my phone to Kyle and see his face turn pale.

Chapter twenty-four

Layla

Zoe and Kyle must have run all the way because they're here in minutes. "Where d'you think she's gone?" Kyle's breathing hard.

"No idea," Mum says. "It's all my fault. I shouldn't have left her alone—"

"It's *not* your fault," I exclaim, glancing at Zoe in alarm.

"Hey." Kyle puts an arm around Mum's shoulders and gives her a hug. "You can't guard her all the time, y'know."

"He's right," Aunty Claire says, then, turning to Kyle, "Your dad and Amber are driving around looking for her, but they've had no luck, either. . ."

"Well," Kyle says, "let's start searching too. Where've you looked so far?"

As I list all the places we've been, my brother's face falls.

"We're running out of ideas," Mum adds.

"We'll look *everywhere*," Zoe says firmly. "We're

bound to find her eventually." Although I'm glad she's here, I feel bad that we're ruining audition day for her.

"You needn't have come," I murmur.

"Of course I had to come! What else would I have done?"

"We'd just about finished anyway," Kyle adds.

"You didn't miss your chance, did you?" I gasp. "Oh, Zoe!"

"I don't care," she says quickly. "To be honest, I didn't want to do it without you anyway. It didn't feel right." She turns as another figure hurries towards us. Ben.

"What's he doing here?" I ask.

He runs over and stops, catching his breath. "I've come to help," he explains. "Zoe, Jude's keeping an eye on Matty, OK? Seeing as Annalise stormed off—"

"Oh, God." Zoe clasps a hand to her mouth. "I can't believe I forgot about Matty again. I just ran out and left him. . ."

"He's fine," Ben says with a smile. "He was playing the drums when I left."

"Well," Mum says, "it's really good of you all to come. How about heading out of town, up towards Gran's old cottage? Maybe she's wandered off in that direction."

"D'you really think she'd go that far?" I ask, frowning. It's a cool, breezy day, and fine rain is starting to fall.

Mum bites her lip. "I don't know, love, but I can't think what else to do." Her eyes fill with tears.

"She'll be OK, Mum," I say, wishing I could believe it myself.

"I'm sure she will, darling. Anyway, Claire and I are going to check the shops again in case we missed her. And if she's not there – well, I'd better call the police and report her as missing. . ."

"Mum," Kyle says firmly, "we'll find her, all right?" He looks round at Zoe, Ben and me. "C'mon, let's go."

No one says anything much as we trudge through the park and follow the narrow lane that leads out to the hills. We know Gran's wearing her flowery pink dress with a rust-coloured cardie over it, which should at least be easy to spot from a distance. I keep scanning each side of the lane, hoping to see a fleck of brightness against the green, and feel terrible for being annoyed when she left her teeth in my mug. Right now I'd give anything to have Gran back home, moaning about her feet or her missing dentures, or insisting on eating a roast dinner in a sandwich.

Ben and Kyle have marched ahead. "We're going to split off," Ben says, glancing back. "I'll make my way towards the quarry and Kyle's going to head over the hills. Does everyone have their mobiles?"

"Yep." Kyle nods.

"I do," Zoe replies.

"I've left mine at home," I say, "but me and Zoe will stick together and head up to Gran's old place. Zoe, you should give them your number—"

"I've got it already," Ben says quickly, clambering over the fence and marching across the field. Sheep scatter in fright as Kyle jogs away in the opposite direction.

I blink at Zoe. "Ben has your number?"

"Yeah." She doesn't meet my eye. "He asked for it at the auditions."

"Oh." So . . . he likes her too. He likes *both* of us . . . or does he really? Maybe he collects girls' numbers, just to make himself look even more popular than he already is? I glance at Zoe as we walk. The silence between us is as heavy as the dark clouds above.

"Zo," I say hesitantly, "do you . . . d'you think it's weird that Ben's asked for both our numbers?"

She glances at me. "Yeah, a bit. I mean, I know you like him—"

"There's stuff I haven't told you about," I cut in.

"What?" she asks, eyes wide.

I bite my lip. "He sort of asked me out – one night when he was staying over at our place. At least, that's what it seemed like at the time. . ."

"Why didn't you say?" she gasps.

"Because I knew you had a crush on him too!"

She laughs, and I could almost cry with relief. "You really thought I'd mind?"

I shrug as we pass the row of cottages huddled at the edge of the woods; they've seen better days, with peeling paint and dirty windows. "I wasn't sure. You had all that stuff happening – being sent to your dad's, and

Annalise arriving. . ."

She turns to me and smiles. "I didn't know what to tell you, either. About Ben asking for my number today, I mean. . ."

The lane is leading us through the woods now, and the faint rain feels like cool breath on my face. "Isn't it crazy?" I say. "We've never kept secrets from each other before. . ."

"And all over a boy," she says with a snigger. "God. What happened to us?"

"Ben," I murmur, linking my arm through Zoe's. "*That's* what happened." It's a horrible day, with Gran being lost. But in a small way, something good's happened too.

We've reached the entrance to Dean House. The "sold" sign is still here and the place looks dark and un-lived-in. Glancing around to check no one's around, we quietly step into the grounds.

"So what's actually happened between you two?" Zoe whispers.

"Nothing! We've just talked, that's all. I'd have told you if there was anything else. . ."

She giggles. "Are you sure?"

I turn and study her face: my best friend in the world. "Yeah," I say. "No more secrets – ever."

"No more secrets," she agrees.

With my arm still linked in hers, I point to the tree house at the far end of the garden. "Remember that?"

"Yeah, I do." She smiles. "We never dared to go in it, did we?"

"Let's go up now," I say, and we run towards it and clamber up the ladder, scrambling in through the narrow doorway.

"Your frog helmet!" Zoe cries, grabbing the shiny green dome. "What's it doing here?"

"Um . . . I left it here that day I went cycling on my own. And . . . Ben showed up—"

"You and Ben were in here together?" Her eyes widen.

"Yeah." I sense myself blushing furiously. But at least I'm being honest at last. . .

"What happened?" Zoe asks.

"Nothing," I say firmly.

"Did he kiss you?"

"No!" I exclaim. "I *promise* he didn't. I'd have told you that. . ." Hang on, would I really? Maybe not. . .

"Layla," she hisses suddenly. "Did you hear that?"

We both fall silent. There's the crunch of tyres on gravel. "Someone's driving into the grounds," I hiss, peering through the tree-house window. A lorry has appeared with "Davenport Removals" on its side.

"People must be moving in," says Zoe. "C'mon – let's go. . ."

We scramble down the ladder and head towards the gates, realizing we'll have to pass the lorry on the way out.

"Hey!" A large, bald man jumps down from the lorry. "This is private property, you know."

"We're looking for my friend's gran," Zoe explains as a second man climbs out. "She used to live out this way."

"Missing, is she?" the bald man asks, his voice softening.

I nod as the other man opens the back of the lorry and starts to lift out polished wooden chairs. "Look," Zoe says, nudging me, "a car's coming."

"They're the new owners," the bald man explains. "We haven't seen anyone on the way, but maybe they have."

Car doors open and a family climbs out: a man, a woman and a girl of around our age. "These girls are looking for a lost grandma," the removal man explains.

"Oh, really?" The woman's face is full of concern. "What's happened?"

"We're not sure," I start to explain. "I'm sorry – I know we shouldn't be here. . ."

"It's OK," the woman says kindly.

My eyes fill with tears and I try to blink them away. "She wanders off sometimes," Zoe tells her. "Kind of forgets where she is. . ." Hearing her saying it out loud causes a wave of sadness to crash over me. I look round at this family: the smartly dressed dad, the kind-looking mum with long auburn hair and the daughter in denim shorts and a big red sweater that clashes – in a good way – with her hair, which matches her mum's.

"Aw, that's like my gran, isn't it, Mum?" the girl says.

"Sounds like it," she replies. "It must be so worrying for you. I do hope you find her."

I swallow. "Thanks. Um ... so you're moving in, then?"

The man smiles. "Yes, finally!"

"Are you coming to our school?" I ask the girl. "Mossbridge High, I mean?"

"Yeah." She smiles. "I was supposed to start straight after Easter but we couldn't move in time."

"We'll look out for you on Monday," Zoe says. "I'm Zoe, this is Layla—"

"And I'm Charlotte," she says.

"See you, then," I say. "We'd better keep searching. . ." They wave and wish us luck.

The sky has darkened now, and there's a rumble of thunder as we make our way along the lane. Using Zoe's phone, I call Mum.

"I've checked every shop," she says glumly, "even the ones she'd never buy anything from. The police have registered her as a missing person."

"Oh, Mum," I cry, "we'll keep looking. . ."

I try to phone Kyle to update him but he doesn't answer; he never does. "Why can't boys use their phones," I grumble, as Zoe's starts ringing in my hand. "Zoe? Layla?" comes the urgent voice.

"It's Layla," I say. "Is that you, Ben?"

"Yeah – listen, you've got to come to the quarry. . ."

"The quarry?" I repeat. "Why?"

"Just come, OK? And *hurry*."

We run all the way, over the fields to the place where Gran used to bring us when we were little. A place for picnics and campfires. A time when she didn't forget things or wander off. My eyes fill with tears as the line of twisted trees comes into view. These mark the top of the quarry. Beyond them is a steep, rocky cliff – a huge hollow in the earth, abandoned for as long as I can remember.

"Layla! Zoe!" Ben is waving at us from between the trees.

"What is it?" I ask, breathless now as we reach him.

"It . . . it might be nothing. . ." He glances back towards the quarry. I step forward and swallow hard.

"What is it?" Zoe exclaims.

Ben opens his mouth as if unsure how to tell us. "I . . . I think there's something down there. . ."

I run towards the edge of the cliff, but hardly dare look. I blink, checking the jagged sides of the quarry and the boulders at the bottom. There's the odd smudge of green where grass has managed to force its way through the rock.

"I can't see anything." My voice comes out as a whisper.

"Neither can I," Zoe murmurs.

Ben stands between us and points. "Look — right down at the bottom. . ."

I narrow my eyes and focus hard. Then I see it — a dash of rusty orange against the grey rocks. "Is that Gran?" I cry out. "It looks like her cardie! The one Mum said she was wearing. . ."

We all stare down. "Oh my God," Zoe breathes.

"Gran!" I yell, my voice cracking. "Gran — is that you?"

Nothing.

"I'm going down to see," I blurt out.

"Layla, you can't," Zoe cries, grabbing my arm. "It's too dangerous. You'll slip and fall. . ."

"Like Gran did. . ." I'm crying now, picturing her wandering out here, maybe trying to get back to her old cottage or our favourite picnic spot.

"I'll go," Ben says, and before we can stop him he's clambering down, causing loose stones to fall with each step. I follow him tentatively, focusing on finding a safe place for each step, and aware of Zoe making her way down behind me.

"Stay up at the top," I call back to her. "This isn't safe—"There's a sound of feet missing their footing and a tumble of rocks. It's not Zoe who's falling, but Ben — tumbling downwards with a startled cry. I'm scrambling as fast as I can, and already I can see it's not Gran lying there in a heap at the bottom, but a fox. Ben has landed beside it with a sharp *crack*. "Ben!" I scream as Zoe and I rush towards him.

He's as still as the dead animal beside him. There's blood on his head, seeping into his light brown hair, and a jagged gash on his cheek. "Are you all right?" I gasp. "Ben – *please* say something." I turn to Zoe. "Look at that cut on his face. . ." It's seeping blood, livid red against the paleness of his cheek.

"Ben, can you hear us?" I crouch down and gently touch his forehead.

"Uhhh. . ." He utters a groan as, slowly, one eye opens. "Layla?" He peers at my face as if amazed to see me here.

"Are you OK? D'you think you've broken something?"

"I . . . dunno." He moves his right leg and flinches with pain. "Yeah, think so. . ."

"We need to get you out of here," Zoe murmurs, pulling her mobile from her pocket. "What's your home number?"

He groans again.

"Ben," I urge him, "we need to phone your parents or an ambulance or the police. . . *Someone* will have to get you out of here. . ."

"No," he mutters.

"But . . ." I glance up at the quarry's steep, jagged sides, "there's no way we'll be able to get you back up there."

I study his lovely face, now smeared with blood and already beginning to swell around the right eye.

"Can I have your phone?" Zoe asks. "If you've forgotten your home number, we can find it in your contacts. . ."

Ben doesn't respond.

"Let me get it," I say, carefully pulling it out of his pocket and peering at the screen. "It's locked, Ben. Can you manage to unlock it for me?"

This time, he shakes his head. "Not my parents," he mutters, real fear shining in his clear blue eyes. "Please, call someone else . . . anyone else."

"They've got to know," I insist. "They'll come and help. . ." Without thinking, I reach out to hold his hand. "Are you worried that they'll be mad at you?"

"You did it for the best reason," Zoe points out. "You were helping to look for Layla's gran. . ."

"Please tell me your home number," I whisper.

The silence seems to stretch for ever. I glance around the quarry, which seemed so amazing when we were little, when we'd sit up at the top, waiting for the fox to come. Sometimes Gran would bring us all here at dusk, when there was a better chance of spotting him. *Foxes are nocturnal*, she explained, *because they like to go about their business in secret.*

Ben touches his face and inspects the blood on his hand. I glance down at the dead creature beside us. It's huge — a burnt-orange colour, and looks perfect, like nothing bad should have happened to it.

"You can't call my parents," Ben says softly.

"Why not?" I don't get it at all.

"I lied. I don't live with them." Fat tears fill his eyes and I squeeze his hand. I've never seen a boy cry before, apart from Jude, when someone accidentally trapped his hand in the door at primary school. This is different. Ben isn't crying because something hurts, like a finger or a foot. He's crying like this is the saddest thing ever.

"I'm sorry," Ben says, "I lied about everything. Nothing I told you is true."

Chapter twenty-five

Zoe

"Right," Mum says when I call her, "listen to me. It's really important that you don't try to move him. . ."

"Yes, Mum," I murmur, wishing she was here right now.

"Is anyone else with you?"

"Just Layla. . ."

"OK – so the two of you keep him calm. You're at the bottom of the quarry, right?"

"Uh-huh. . ."

"I'll leave Matty with Annalise," she goes on. "I'll call an ambulance, and I'll be with you myself in a few minutes. . ." Even though I know she deals with emergencies every day, I'm still amazed at how calm she is.

"You mean *you're* coming?" I exclaim.

"Of course I am, darling. I'll probably be there before the ambulance. . . Now, look after Ben, keep talking to him, keep him alert – and I'll be with you as soon as I can."

So we sit and wait and, rather than asking what he lied about exactly, we talk about the fox. "Why do people hate them so much?" I murmur.

"It doesn't seem fair," Layla agrees. "I mean, I know they kill chickens and stuff, but that's just to survive, isn't it?"

She breaks off as Ben mumbles something we don't quite catch. "They have a reputation," he offers, more clearly this time.

"Yeah." I nod. "People think they just want to cause trouble. . ."

"When they're just trying to live their life," Ben adds. I look at him, wanting to ask so much. Then, as if reading my question hanging in the air between us, he adds, "Things didn't work out with my parents so they sent me to live with my aunt."

"Oh," I whisper, glancing at Layla. *Why did you lie then?* I want to ask. *What were you trying to prove?*

Mum's voice cuts through the damp spring air. "Careful!" I call up as she makes her way towards us, somehow managing to step on only the solid rocks, the ones which don't shift or send a shower of stones tumbling down towards us.

"Ben," she says, crouching beside him. "That's a nasty cut on your face – but don't worry. The nearest hospital's not too far away. . ."

"Mum works there," I add.

"I'm Alison," she says gently. "I'm a surgeon—"

"Will I need surgery?" Ben exclaims.

"Don't worry, whatever happens you'll be in good hands." I watch her hands as she gently lifts away a strand of hair that's stuck to the blood on Ben's cheek. "I'll come to hospital with you," she adds. "Have your parents been told what's happened?"

He shakes his head. "It's complicated."

"But they *have* to know. . ."

"Ben lives with his aunt," I explain.

"Has anyone called her?"

He sighs heavily. "Aunt Mary doesn't have a phone."

"So where does she. . . ?" Mum trails off. "Oh, never mind. We'll get in touch with her somehow. Zoe, d'you think you and Layla can climb back up safely?"

"Yes, of course. . ."

"Off you go then," she says. "And, Ben, don't worry – you'll be out of here very soon."

Layla and I don't talk as we make our way up towards the trees. When we stop and glance back, Mum and Ben seem a long, long way down. The only sounds are the swish of branches and the rustle of a bird in the undergrowth.

Then another sound breaks through the stillness – a whirr, growing louder and louder, the black speck not a bird but a helicopter, turning in a wide arc. At first I assume it'll land in the field, but it tips on its side and soars down over the edge of the quarry, sending up clouds of grey dust. Layla and I watch in silence as two men jump out. Ben is lifted onto a stretcher and carried into the helicopter, followed by Mum.

Within seconds, it's taken off again, and the boy we know nothing about is soaring above our heads against a dark metal sky. We stand by the twisted trees and watch until the helicopter's out of sight.

It turns out that Layla's gran's adventure didn't take her out into the hills after all. She'd just strolled through town and gone into the old ladies' boutique – the one that had thrown out the shop dummy whose arm Matty had brought home to torment me with in the holidays. It's one of those shops where they only see a customer about twice a week, so who can blame the woman who works in there for dozing at the till? She wasn't even aware of Layla's gran choosing an armful of cardigans to try on, and slipping into the changing room.

"Apparently, she only discovered Gran when she was about to lock up, and noticed a pair of feet in the gap under the curtain." Layla's mum can laugh about it now. "You must have been in there *hours*, Mum."

"Well," Layla's gran retorts, "I'm not good at choosing colours. Not like Layla. And I just couldn't decide."

"I can't believe no one knew you were in there," Kyle says, shaking his head. His gran chuckles as if this has all been a fuss over nothing. We've agreed not to mention that one of our friends – can we even call Ben that now, a *real* friend, I mean? – fell down the quarry because of her, and that my mum's still at the hospital with him now.

As Layla helps her mum make a stack of sandwiches in the kitchen, Kyle appears by my side. "Pretty dramatic day, huh?"

I smile. "Can't believe we mistook a dead fox for your gran's cardie."

We plonk ourselves down on the sofa in the living room. "Yeah. I'm glad you're OK, though. You were lucky. . ." Kyle's eyes meet mine, and out of nowhere, my long-ago crush flickers back into life. I thought I'd got over that. Crushes on best friends' brothers aren't allowed, I kept telling myself.

"That quarry's really dangerous," he adds.

I nod. "Well, we didn't have much choice."

"Yeah, I know. Anyway, at least Gran turned up. God, Zoe – my family. I hope you realize how normal yours is." He laughs, sending a cloud of butterflies fluttering around my stomach.

"You really thinks so?" I ask. "What about Annalise?"

"Yeah, but she's not family, is she? She doesn't count."

I sigh and check the clock on the living-room wall. "Well, Mum seems to think she's great."

Kyle gives me a wry smile.

"Anyway," I add, "speaking of Annalise ... she's

looking after Matty right now, and they're not exactly the best of friends, so I'd better go."

There's a flurry of hugs as I leave – even from Kyle, which causes my heart to flip over. I'm sure it doesn't mean anything. He's probably just relieved that his gran's been found.

Even so, I can't keep the mile-wide grin off my face as I run home.

Chapter twenty-six

Layla

I can't sleep for thinking about Ben. *Nothing I told you is true*, he told us. What did he mean? That his dad doesn't work in the music business? That he didn't go to boarding school? I sit up in bed, pulling my duvet around me like a cape. 3.21 a.m, the clock says. I feel chilled to the bone.

Danny, Harris and Jude showed up at our house soon after Gran had been found, and we told them what Ben said about his parents. "There must've been some reason why he lied," Kyle suggested, while Harris claimed he'd known all along that Ben just wanted to be the centre of attention. "It was better before he came here," he announced.

Do I believe that? I'm not sure. Nothing ever happened in this town, and now it has.

Jude was the only one who didn't say much when all of this was being discussed. In the morning I run into him on the landing. I'm wearing my scruffiest T-shirt and my oldest jeans. He's a bit quiet and bleary-eyed.

"Did everyone stay over last night?" I ask.

"Yeah." He smiles. "You're up early. . ."

I nod. "Couldn't really sleep last night—"

"Look," he says, pointing to the angry-looking bruise on my arm. "You hurt yourself."

"Yeah, must have happened yesterday. I didn't notice it at the time. . ."

"Too much other stuff going on?" he suggests.

"Just a bit." I shrug. There's a pause, but it doesn't feel awkward between us. I want to tell Jude how impressed I am about how he's handled the whole Ben thing. But now Kyle's calling him back into his room, saying, "Jude, you've got to see this! It's meant to be the scariest film ever made. . ."

Jude rolls his eyes at me and laughs. "A horror film, first thing in the morning? I hate them anyway. . ."

"You hate horror films? I never knew that!"

He nods and laughs. "I'm always a bit envious of you and Zoe, to be honest – holed up in your room, watching a comedy. . ."

"Really? Well, next time, come watch it with us." As Jude's face lights up, it dawns on me how I'd love that. I've never felt tense or self-conscious around him.

"Layla?" Mum calls up. "Zoe's here!"

It feels too hectic in the kitchen, what with Gran and Mum busying about, and the screams from the film are kind of off-putting in my room, so Zoe and I head to the park. She fills me in on what's happened overnight. "Ben's broken an ankle and his right arm," she tells me, "so he won't be playing guitar any time soon."

"He'll hate that," I murmur as we install ourselves on a bench.

"Yeah, well, Mum says he's lucky it wasn't worse. That cut on his face was pretty bad, but she treated him herself. . ."

"What did she have to do?"

Zoe smiles. "Nothing with cow skin. Just stitches — it was a really ragged wound, though, so it took her ages. . ." She breaks off. "He'll have a scar."

"Really?" I try to picture his face, and it's a little less vivid already. "Scars are nice," I add.

"Interesting," Zoe agrees.

We make our way towards the swings, which are still damp with dew, and start swaying gently back and forth. "Mum managed to track down his aunt," she adds. "She phoned around until she found someone who knows her, and they drove out to her place to tell her what'd happened. Can you believe she doesn't have a phone? Anyway, she visited him in hospital last night."

"Where does she live?" I ask.

"Out in the hills, way past Dean House, down a lane that doesn't go anywhere else, Mum said. It's called Rowan Cottage. Ever seen it?"

"Don't think so," I say, jumping down onto the soft, springy grass. "But how about having a look?"

We set off on this crisp, bright Sunday morning before our town has properly woken up. There's the sound of power saws as we speed past Dean House, and someone's inside the tree house, hammering away.

"Hope they're not taking it down," Zoe muses.

"Me too," I say, feeling a little nervous all of a sudden. Neither of us has talked about why we're doing this, or what we'll say when we get there. It just seemed like the right thing to do.

Now, though, as we turn into the lane and spot the tiny white cottage in the distance, I'm not so sure.

There's no bell or knocker so I just rap on the door. The door is so old and worn there's hardly any paint left on it, and the small window beside it is cracked. We're miles from town now. I check my phone; there's not even a signal out here.

"Maybe we should go back?" Zoe whispers.

"No – c'mon, we have to find out what's been going on." I knock again, harder this time. My breath catches in my throat as the door opens.

"Yes?" A small, thin woman is standing before us. Her fine brown hair is pulled back into a messy ponytail, and her pale blue eyes are guarded.

I clear my throat. "Erm . . . hope you don't mind us just dropping by. We're friends of Ben's—"

234

"Are you his Aunt Mary?" Zoe asks in a timid voice.

Her face softens. "Yes, I am."

"Erm," I start, "we were with him yesterday when he had the accident. . ."

"Oh." She blinks at us, as if not quite knowing what to do next.

"And we wondered how he is," Zoe murmurs.

Mary musters the tiniest smile. "Come in," she says.

Zoe and I glance at each other, and she edges closer to me as we follow Mary into the cottage. The windows are so dirty daylight barely struggles through, but there's something cosy about the place. The living room is even smaller than ours, and crammed with too much furniture. The old, worn-out sofa is strewn with brightly coloured cushions, and three guitars gleam from their stands in the corner.

"Are they Ben's?" I ask.

"Yes, of course," Mary says. "I can't play a thing. I love to hear him play, though. That's what I'll miss when he leaves." She motions for us to sit down and settles into the armchair opposite.

"He's leaving?" Zoe asks.

Mary nods.

"Where's he going?"

"We're not sure yet," she says. "We still have to sort things out."

I look at Zoe, wondering how to find out what we need to know. "And, er, how *is* he?" I ask tentatively.

"He's doing fine," she starts. "He's broken his ankle and arm, of course, but the main worry was that terrible cut on his face. Luckily, the paediatric surgeon was there and did an amazing job at stitching it. She's one of the best in the country, apparently. . ."

"That's my mum," Zoe says, flushing a little.

Mary's eyes widen. "Really?"

Zoe nods, and this snippet of information seems to make Mary relax.

"I gather, from the doctor – your mum, I mean – that Ben hadn't told anyone he lives with me."

We both shake our heads and wait for her to explain.

"The thing is, Benedict's had a difficult time. . ."

"*Benedict?*" I exclaim.

Mary smiles wryly. "I know he prefers to be called Ben. His parents don't like it, though . . . well, they don't like a lot of things."

So many questions are milling round in my head, I don't know what to ask first. "Is Ben's dad in the music business?" I blurt out.

"No," she says with a laugh. "What made you think that?"

"Er . . . no reason," Zoe says, unconvincingly.

Mary shakes her head. "Benedict's – *Ben's* – father is the deputy head teacher at his old school. . ."

"Boarding school?" I ask.

"It's a boarding school, yes, but Ben was a day pupil there, like his two older brothers. It's one of the top private schools in the country."

I nod, taking this in. "Why did he leave?" I ask.

Mary presses her lips together, as if unsure how much to tell us. "He was *asked* to leave."

"You mean suspended?" I ask.

"Temporarily, yes. But you can imagine how awkward this was for his father. You see, Ben's brothers had been top students. The whole family's very academic. Their fathe, my brother – was a pupil there too. Sorley College is a huge part of their lives." She tugs out her ponytail and rakes at her hair with her fingers.

"So why was he suspended?" Zoe asks.

"It wasn't his fault," she says firmly. "That school was completely wrong for him, I always said. Exams, exams, exams. Nothing else mattered. Can you imagine being viewed as a perpetual disappointment? You know how creative he is. No wonder he wanted to stir things up. . ."

What did he do, *though?* I'm not sure if it's OK to ask.

"So, after he was suspended," I say hesitantly, "what happened next?"

Mary exhales. "Well, it was very embarrassing for his father, of course. He fought to keep Ben in the school, but there was only so much he could do without it looking like favouritism. But he couldn't forgive him for it. Said it had damaged the family's reputation, and from then on, things went downhill at home. They *couldn't* live together. . ." She tails off and regards us sadly.

"So he came here," Zoe prompts her.

Mary nods. "He needed a fresh start."

"Did you want him to?" I ask.

She pauses, as if unsure how to answer. "He is a good boy, you know. Helpful, did lots of errands for me. And the company was nice. . ." She looks first at Zoe, then me. "The thing is," she adds, "he doesn't have anyone else."

Silence fills the room. Now I *sort of* get it – how desperate he was to fit in around here. In a small way, I know how hard that can be. Ben needed a fresh start, Mary said, and he used moving here as a chance to reinvent himself. Don't I want to do that too sometimes? I mean, how often have I imagined having Zoe's life, with her gorgeous bedroom and balcony overlooking a garden, and not a stinky back yard?

As we say bye to Mary, I still don't understand everything. But I know I'm going to try.

Chapter twenty-seven

Zoe

My little brother is hiding again. "Matty!" Annalise calls up from the bottom of the stairs. "Hurry up, would you?" She plonks a hand on her hip. There's a sore-looking bit on her left ankle from where the strap of her platform sandal's been rubbing. "That stupid boy," she grumbles, marching back to the kitchen and flinging open the fridge, where nothing seems to please her. I'm sure she exists on the stash of crisps and biscuits she keeps in her room. "He's driving me mad," she mutters. "God, this had better be worth it."

"What d'you mean?" I ask.

"Nothing."

I glance at the kitchen doorway, willing him to come down so she doesn't get even more annoyed. Annalise seems different today, though. Not shouty, like she was at the auditions, or when Matty played his Oreo prank.

This is a quieter, simmering annoyance, and for some reason, it's scarier.

It's me who finds him, cross-legged on the floor behind his bedroom curtain. "Matty, what's wrong?"

"Don't wanna go to school," he mutters.

"C'mon," I say. "You've *got* to go."

"Wanna stay here," he mutters.

I frown at my brother. He looks flat on this grey Monday morning, like some of the fizz has gone out of him. "You don't want to stay at home with her, do you?" I whisper.

"I wanna stay home with Fanta." He gets up from the floor and plonks himself on his unmade bed, facing his fish tank.

"Matty, come *on*. We're going to be late and Annalise is acting weird today. . ."

He frowns at me. "How weird?"

I shrug. "Don't know. Just quiet and sort of . . . *brooding*." I take hold of his hand. "Please, Matty. . ." He doesn't need to be asked again. Thankfully, he's already dressed, and he jams a cold slice of toast into his mouth before we head off to school.

"Have a nice day," Annalise calls after us, in such a fake-happy voice that Matty and I can't help smirking in the garden.

"*Have a nice day*," he keeps mimicking all the way to school, making me laugh every time. I never thought I'd say this, but sometimes I'm glad to have a little brother like him. He's not scared of our weird, newly ginger-headed au pair. Bet he's already planning his next prank to play on her. I can almost hear his brain whirring away as I drop him at school, and surprise him with a hug at the gates.

"Hey," he yells, shoving me off.

"*Have a nice day!*" I sing-song, hurrying off to meet Layla. She's waiting on the corner as usual, and the smile bursts across her face when she sees me.

"Ben called Kyle," she announces. "He's feeling much better. He's had operations on his ankle and arm, and he says your mum did an amazing job at stitching his face. He had concussion too, so they want to keep an eye on him, but he'll be allowed home pretty soon."

"That's great." I glance at her, avoiding looking at CJ across the street. "Where's home, though? It didn't sound like he's going back to Mary's."

"Think he'll go to his parents'?"

"Don't know. Sounds like he's not really wanted there, either."

We fall into silence, and I can tell she's thinking the same as me: who cares if he lied? I can't imagine not being wanted at home. Sure, I wish Mum and Dad were still together, and that I didn't have to spend my visits to Dad's watching Olivia cantering around the paddock. Ideally, I'd prefer not to have an au pair, and for Mum not to work so much – but then, she *is* brilliant at what she does. Didn't Ben's Aunt Mary say so?

We're at school now, and already the place feels different without Ben, even though he was only here for a few days before the accident. It's like when you drop a Mentos mint into a bottle of Coke and it goes *whooosh!* An instant reaction.

"Shame about what happened to Ben." CJ has sidled up to Layla and me outside the school office.

"Yeah, I know," I say, not wanting to discuss it with her. She looks different, though. Less hard, despite her stony expression. "You sang really well at the audition," I add.

She flushes. "Thanks."

"I didn't know you could sing," I continue. "I mean, you were never in the choir or anything—"

"No, well, my mum wouldn't let me go," she says flatly.

"Why not?" Layla asks.

CJ shrugs. "She thought it was a waste of time. And it costed, didn't it?"

"Not much," I remark. "Just a couple of pounds a week for Acorn funds. . ."

"Yeah, but you all had new clothes for concerts and stuff. Black trousers, white shirts—"

I glance down, realizing I'd never noticed how greying her school shirts are, and how her skirt hangs limply, even though she's tried to roll it over at her waist to shorten it. "Mum's not really into us doing stuff," she adds. "Not like yours."

Does she mean I'm spoiled? I don't think so. . .

"Well," I say quickly, "I hope you're going to sing at the concert. You really should, you know. You were easily the best. . ."

"It won't happen now, will it?" CJ remarks. "Ben's broken his arm and won't be able to play guitar for months."

"No," I cut in, "it *has* to go ahead. It was a brilliant idea and if we can persuade Kyle and the others to go ahead. . ." I look around and spot Jude. "You'll do it, won't you?" I call across as the bell rings.

"Do what?" he asks, looking startled.

"The concert at the Acorn—"

"Excuse me!" Miss Baker, our gym teacher, raises her voice and stares pointedly at the clock on the wall. "Can I just remind you that the bell has gone, and that this isn't just a social gathering? Move along – you have classes to get to."

Matty chatters all the way home. It's hard to pay attention as I'm wondering what Ben's doing now – not in an *oh-my-God-this-crush-is-taking-over-my-brain* kind of way. More in a concerned way, really.

Is he still lying in a hospital bed right now, all alone? Will Mary visit him again? When Matty broke his arm, the nurses brought out a fold-out bed so Mum could sleep beside him the night he had to stay over. He was *never* alone – not for a minute.

All's quiet when we get home. Annalise is lying on the sofa, flipping idly through a celeb magazine, and doesn't even look up when we walk in.

"Hi," I say, remembering that I'm meant to be making an effort with her.

"Hi," she says without shifting her gaze from the page. With a grunt, Matty clatters upstairs.

Although I'd rather head up to my room myself, it feels a bit unfriendly, so I perch on the sofa next to her and try to think of something to say.

"*Nooooo!!!*" comes the scream.

"Matty, what's wrong?" I leap up, tear upstairs and into his bedroom.

He is sobbing, face down on his bed. Crying like I've never heard him cry before.

"Matty, what happened?" I land on the bed beside him. He's crying too hard to answer. "Please tell me. . ."

He sobs and gulps until, finally, he turns towards me. He looks awful – red-faced, with his hair plastered to his wet cheeks. "Look," he whispers, pointing towards Fanta's bowl. There's just the little plastic tree and the bridge and the Aztec pyramid thing. No Fanta. At first, I think his goldfish is hiding, playing a little prank of his own. But there's nowhere he could be.

"Where's Fanta?" I ask.

"He's gone!" comes my brother's tiny voice. "I think a cat came in again."

"But. . ." I look around the room. "The window's not open, Matty."

I get up and look down on the garden below. A cat couldn't have got in. So Fanta hasn't been eaten. It's a mystery. Unless. . . "Hang on a minute," I murmur, padding lightly downstairs.

In the living room, Annalise has flung her magazine on the floor and is now picking at her fingernails with a kirby grip. "What happened to Fanta?" I ask calmly.

"What?" She squints at me.

"*Fanta.* Matty's fish."

She carries on jabbing at her nails. "It was just a fish, Zoe. A stupid fish he won at Baxter Valley that wasn't gonna live long anyway."

"What've you done to Fanta?" My voice has risen to a shriek. Matty's standing at the bottom of the stairs now, his eyes red and puffy and his hair all poking up.

She laughs a horrible, mean little laugh and drops the kirby grip onto our glass coffee table. "You're pretty keen on pranking me," she says, glaring at my brother, "so I thought I'd get you back."

"What?" Matty cries.

"You can't do that—" I start.

"Where did you put him?" Matty demands, cheeks red with fury. "Give him back!"

Annalise smirks, getting up from the sofa and drifting into the kitchen, where she fills the kettle. "I can't," she says, "'cause he's in the loo."

"You flushed him down the loo?" I yell as Matty's face crumples again.

"Yeah."

"But . . . why? Because of the Oreo thing? That's a horrible thing to do!"

Annalise shrugs.

"You're so mean," I yell as Matty runs off to check all our bathrooms. "I *hate* you. I wish you'd never come—"

The front door flies open and Mum is standing there. "What is going here?" she barks. Annalise and I turn to face her.

"She flushed Fanta down the loo," Matty announces, reappearing briefly then clattering back upstairs.

Mum sets down her bag on the floor. Her short hair is growing out and the shadows beneath her eyes look particular dark in her paler-than-usual face. "Can someone tell me what's going on?"

"Annalise put Fanta in the toilet," I say flatly. "To get Matty back for the Oreo trick."

Mum's eyes widen. "Seriously?"

"Yeah. . ."

Mum shakes her head slowly and glares at Annalise. We can hear Matty, running back and forth across the landing, announcing that his pet is nowhere to be seen. "What on earth possessed you to do that?" Mum splutters.

Annalise sniffs loudly. "I don't know what you're talking about. A cat. . ."

"She just admitted it, Mum. And the window was shut," I shout.

"It was Matty's pet," Mum exclaims. "What made you do such a mean thing?"

"Look—"

"No," Mum cuts in, "don't tell me – I don't want to hear any excuses, Annalise. I can't have you live here with my children any more. You can make some calls tonight and sort out arrangements, and I'll be taking you to the station first thing tomorrow. . ."

"No, not again!" she exclaims.

We both peer at her. "What d'you mean by that?" Mum asks.

"Nothing." She glares at us as Matty mooches in. "Oh, I don't suppose *you* care. I only took this job 'cause Daddy said it was my last chance—"

"At what?" I ask, completely baffled.

She looks me right in the eye. "Last chance to hang on to my allowance. Thanks to you lot, it'll be stopped."

"Is that like pocket money?" Matty asks, his eyes still pink and sore.

"Ha," she snorts. "I'd imagine it's a *bit* more than that. You didn't think I could live on what you pay me, do you?"

"But—" Mum starts.

"Anyway," Annalise cuts in, "he was annoyed that I haven't managed to stick at a job, so I took this one to keep him happy. He said, as long as I could hold down a job for at least six months, then he'd keep putting money into my account. . ." She looks around at us all, her eyes narrowed and mean. "You didn't think I *wanted* to be an au pair, did you?"

We stand there in silence. Even Matty is speechless. Then finally, he turns to Mum and takes her hand. "Fanta's gone," he mutters. "She flushed him away. He's probably dead in a sewer or something."

Mum pulls him close, shutting her eyes for a moment. "Just go," she says under her breath.

"But what'll I tell Daddy?"

I've never heard Mum sound so icy. "Just go to your room, Annalise, and pack your things and leave my family alone."

That night, after Matty's finally been persuaded to go to bed, Mum and I sit up chatting in the kitchen. We don't normally do this. She's too worried that my grades will plummet if I go to bed a second later than ten o'clock. Tonight feels different, though. There's so much to talk about, and it's as if she's forgotten about the time or even that there's school in the morning.

We talk about Annalise, and how Mum feels so responsible. She knew she was using her make-up and perfume, but had figured that she'd give her time to settle in with us before laying down a few rules.

"I've handled this really badly," she sighs. "There were so many signs and I just tried to ignore them. . ."

"It's all right," I say. "It's not your fault. You thought it was the best thing for us. . ."

She shakes her head. "I need to contact Jacqui, who sent me that reference. I can't understand why she was so positive about her. Oh, sweetheart," she adds, hugging me, "I feel terrible, you know? I was too preoccupied to check her out properly."

"Stop blaming yourself, Mum," I say.

She pulls back to study my face. "Forgive me?"

"Of course I do! There's nothing to forgive."

We fall into silence, then she adds, "Now, up to bed, love. It's awfully late."

It's Annalise I'm thinking about as I clean my teeth upstairs. What made her take an au pair job when she obviously doesn't like kids? I don't get it at all.

Ben creeps into my mind too. I know he's fifteen but I hope someone's with him in hospital. I know I'd want Mum or Dad to be with me. I splash my face with water and pat it dry with a towel. And that's when I see it – a little flicker of orange, swimming around in the loo.

So it's not true that fairground fish are weak and die quickly. Fanta has swum back up. He's survived.

Chapter twenty-eight

Layla

I'm meant to be good at putting outfits together. But today, I can't get it right. I try on skirts and shorts and about thirty different tops, while Amber perches on the edge of the top bunk, watching intently as if she's at a fashion show.

"That looks nice," she offers as I check my reflection.

I glance down at the flowery top, the patched denim shorts and the purple tights. "Nope."

"It does, honest!"

But the clothes are already off and I'm pulling on jeans and a plain red T-shirt. "That's boring," Amber remarks.

I sigh heavily. "Yeah, I know."

"You can't go on stage in boring clothes. No one will *notice* you."

I turn and smile at her. "Maybe I don't want to be noticed today."

She wrinkles her freckly nose, not understanding. "Why are you doing it then?"

"'Cause Zoe is."

"Is Zoe too scared to sing by herself?"

"Um . . . I don't think so. But it's what we agreed – that we'd do this together. And I can't let her down."

Amber stretches the elasticated necklace she's wearing and lets it go with a ping. "You're nervous, I can tell."

Of course I am. It's been two weeks since Ben's accident, and Zoe and I have spent every spare moment practising our song. It doesn't matter that we didn't audition – the boys heard us practise for the auditions loads. They're all back together again, as a band: Kyle, Danny, Jude and even Harris, whose contribution still seems to be standing there, looking all thoughtful and telling them what he thinks.

Hell, the jeans and T-shirt will have to do. I pull a comb through my curls and march out of our room. "Can't wait to watch you singing," Amber yells after me.

"Don't put me off, OK?" I call back, running downstairs, realizing I should already be at the Acorn. The boys are there, and Zoe and I had promised to help them set up.

"Layla?" Mum calls from the kitchen. "Something's arrived for you. . ."

"What d'you mean, *something's arrived*?"

"Look," she says, handing me a squishy Jiffy bag. It hasn't come in the post – not on a Saturday afternoon –

and anyway, there's no address, or even a surname. Someone's just written "FOR LAYLA" on the front. Mum grins, clearly as intrigued as I am. "It must have been hand-delivered," she adds. "I went out to put some newspapers in the recycling bin, and there it was."

Weird.

"You didn't see who put it there?"

Mum shakes her head.

"And no one knocked?"

"Not that I heard. Aren't you going to open it, then?"

Amber appears as I peel off the tape. I never get parcels apart from at Christmas and birthdays, and for one horrible moment I wonder if it's someone's idea of a joke. But when I peer inside, there's a small bundle of peacock-blue fabric in there. I pull it out and hold it up. "It's the dress from the vintage market!" I gasp. "I was trying it on and. . ." I tail off, deciding to spare her the details. There are some things she's better off *not* knowing.

"It's lovely," Mum murmurs. "Did someone buy it for you?"

"Honestly, I've no idea. . ." I gaze at the dress, noticing that the rip's been fixed with perfect tiny stitches.

"Was it Zoe?" Mum suggests.

"No, she wasn't there that day. . ." So who *was* it? Could it possibly be someone who wants to say sorry for lying, for pretending to be someone he's not? We've heard that Ben's out of hospital now, recovering at home.

I assume that means he's still at Mary's. . . Conscious of Mum and Amber's eyes boring into me (can't a person get *any* privacy around here?), I peer into the empty Jiffy bag. Only, it's not empty. There's a small square of white paper – a note that says, "GOOD LUCK WITH THE SHOW." And that's it. With a grin, I hurry back up to my room, pull off my boring old jeans and T-shirt and slip on the dress.

This time, the zip doesn't stick. In fact it fits perfectly, like it was made for me.

Zoe is already at the Acorn when I arrive, and the band is setting up. "I love your dress," she exclaims. "Where'd you get it?"

"It just arrived," I say, and fill her in on the mysterious package.

"So who *was* it?"

"Honestly, I've no idea!"

"Well, it's gorgeous," she says, looking great herself in a cherry-red dress with a hint of sparkle. She hardly ever wears a dress, so she's definitely made a big effort today. When I catch her glancing at Kyle, I smile to myself. There's something between them – a kind of spark. How would I feel if Zoe started going out with my brother? I knew she liked him ages ago, although she kept saying I was out of my mind to even *think* it. But now there's no pretending. . .

"You two look great," he says, coming over to fix up

the mics. Only, he's really talking about my best friend, and that's fine. I mean, for a big brother, he's not so bad.

"Are we going to run through the song?" she asks, looking flustered now.

"No," he replies, "there isn't time. What we were thinking is, we'll play our songs, and then the other singers can come on and you two'll be last . . . does that sound OK?"

"Fine," I say, trying to sound casual, as if I do this kind of thing every Saturday night. He wanders back to his drum kit.

"Weird, isn't it?" Zoe murmurs. "I mean, all of this was Ben's idea and he's not even here."

I nod. "I'm sort of glad." I catch Jude's eye as he tunes his guitar in the corner, and he smiles, making my heart flip over. "That Jude's playing again, I mean," I add.

Zoe giggles. "Bet you are. . ."

"Stop it," I snigger, glancing at the rows of empty chairs and wondering if anyone will actually turn up tonight. No, better not think like that.

"Feeling nervous?" Jude is at my side now.

"No, I'm OK." I laugh. "Well, yeah, just a bit. How about you?"

"I'm fine," he says, green eyes shining. "Er, no – actually I'm bloody terrified." He laughs and sweeps back his light brown hair. "It'll be all right, though. It's all about raising money, isn't it? It's a good thing we're doing. . ."

"Well, I hope so," I say as CJ wanders in, arranges herself in a chair on the front row and starts tapping away on her phone. Harris is positioned at the door, ready to sell tickets, and Zoe and I take seats at the side of the stage. CJ's mates have arrived in a sniggering group, and now parents are drifting in too, filling the empty plastic chairs and facing the stage expectantly.

There's Danny and Jude's parents, looking all excited and waving at their boys like they're in a school nativity. I catch Jude's eye and he laughs. He thinks *his* parents are embarrassing? Wait till my family turns up. Gran will probably start showing everyone her feet.

I look down at my dress, then back at Jude. And all of a sudden, I realize – of course, he was with me that day, goofing around and trying on hats at the market. I point at my dress. *Did you. . . ?* I mouth across the stage.

His shy smile says it all.

"Thank you," I call across at him, although I'm not sure he hears me because the theatre's filling up, with only a few empty seats left. Hang on ... where's *my* family?

"Layla," Zoe whispers at my side. "*Look.*" I follow her gaze to where her mum and dad have arrived together.

"They're both here!" I exclaim. "I thought they didn't have anything to do with each other?"

She shakes her head in bewilderment. "God knows what's going on." They don't exactly look relaxed as they find spare seats, but they're here, with Matty, who grabs the chair between them. It doesn't look as if they'll ever get another au pair – not after Zoe's mum tracked down Jacqui, who'd supposedly emailed that glowing reference, and found out that Annalise had written it herself. Annalise hadn't even worked for Jacqui. She was just a family friend. I can't understand how anyone can spout so many lies. . .

Now Mum, Dad, Gran and Amber are all hurrying in – the last people to arrive, of course. There's lots of shuffling as people move up so they can all sit together, just in time. . . The lights go down.

There's a short speech before the band starts playing. It's given by the man who's something high up in the running of the theatre – the one who used to tell me and Zoe off when we giggled during choir practice. But I don't know what he's saying now. I'm too nervous to take anything in. This isn't like singing in the choir, or the concerts at school, when I always felt fairly confident. Today, somehow, the stakes feel much higher. Zoe glances at me, and I try to give her a big, brave smile, but it falters.

"We'll be all right," she whispers. "Remember what Jude said about why we're doing this. . ."

I nod and glance up at the ceiling. It's all cracked and there are mottled stains where water's seeped through. "We can do it," I whisper back.

"Sure we can."

The band launches into their first song. I'm glad Kyle

persuaded the boys to do this after all, when it became clear that Ben would no longer be part of it. They sound confident and together, with only the occasional wrong note, which no one notices anyway as Jude's voice carries the song brilliantly.

In fact, I'm so transfixed by watching him perform that my nerves float away. I'm fine. I *can* do this. They perform three more songs, then Jude announces, "As you know, we have some guest singers tonight. . ."

First up is Jessie, her golden hair gleaming under the lights. "Go, Jessie!" someone yells from the front row. The band plays quietly, allowing her voice to shine out. She's nervous, and her voice wobbles a bit, and when the song's over her face is awash with relief. More singers follow, everyone receiving a huge burst of applause. I feel proud, being part of this, and I haven't even done anything yet.

CJ is onstage now, looking a little out of place in her khaki shorts and an old grey T-shirt that looks too small for her. But as she hits her first note, the whole theatre is awestruck.

"She's amazing," Zoe whispers, and I can only nod in response.

At the end of her song, everyone leaps up onto their feet. I'm clapping madly, and I scan the audience for her parents or her big sister Toni. But none of them have come.

Finally it's our turn – Zoe and me. My stomach

performs a somersault as I stand up and walk towards one of the mics. I glance around at the band, then at Zoe, and back over my shoulder towards Jude. He raises a brow, in a *you-can-do-this* kind of way. I blink down at the shimmering blue of my dress, then at my family. Mum, Dad and Gran are all smiling, waiting. Amber's home-made necklace glints under the lights. The song begins, and our voices ring out – clear and perfectly in tune, like it's just the two of us practising harmonies on Zoe's balcony.

I glance towards the back of the theatre, where a boy has appeared – a boy with a wide, wide smile and his arm in a sling. He stands there for a moment, taking it all in, as if he really shouldn't be here at all.

Then he's gone.

Chapter twenty-nine

Zoe

We see Ben one more time as we're making our way into school on a bright, sunny morning in May. He arrives with a smart-looking woman with her light brown hair coiled neatly into a French plait and a man in a dark grey suit with shoes so shiny they look fresh out of the shop.

"Just a minute," Ben says, breaking away to join me and Layla as we step through the main door. The man and woman follow close behind.

"Are you starting back today?" I ask. "I thought you were moving somewhere else."

"Um ... yeah, I am. Just have some things to pick up from my locker." I nod, trying not to study his face. But it's impossible not to. It's a beautiful face, though it doesn't cause my heart to race now. Not because of the scar, a barely-there comma across his cheek – if anything, it makes him more interesting. No, I mean because I'm over him now. My crush faded. In its place, my old one for Kyle has resurfaced, like fish legend Fanta. In fact, it's more than a crush.

Sometimes it's just the two of us – Kyle and me – but mostly we're in a big gang with Layla, Jude, Harris and Danny – even CJ sometimes, and Charlotte, the girl who moved into Dean House. As well as the park, we also hang out in the tree house in her garden. It has a proper window now, and a carpet. If people think my house is posh, it's nothing compared to her place, which is all done up now and looks amazing.

Of course, none of this would have happened without Ben. In science, we learned about catalysts and how they change things, make things happen, just like he did.

"Are you going back to your old school?" I ask as we make our way towards the lockers together.

"No," he says. "I've persuaded Mum and Dad to let me go to a kind of arts and music school." He smiles bashfully. "Um . . . that's true, by the way."

"You mean, you'll get to play guitar all the time?" Layla asks.

He laughs, aware of his parents, growing impatient a couple of metres away. His mum rolls her eyes and his dad checks his watch, even though there's a huge clock on the wall beside them. "Not exactly. There'll be a bit of maths and science and stuff, but hopefully it won't get in the way too much."

"Benedict?" His mum's voice cuts through the noise of everyone pouring into school. "Could you hurry up and get your things, please?"

"Benedict?" I repeat, trying not to smile.

"Er, only my parents call me that," he says quickly. "Anyway, better go." He strides towards them, looking back just once. "I meant to say, your mum did a great job," he adds.

"She's the best," I say, not caring who hears – not even CJ, who's running into school now, her regulation grey skirt worn with bright red non-uniform tights. She looks good – quirky and different. I think she's copying Layla's style a little bit. She hasn't called me Cow Face since the auditions, and she's said she might even join the drama club that's starting up at the Acorn, once the renovations are finished.

Jude strides in as the bell goes, his rucksack slung over his shoulder. He grins and waves, and I catch CJ glancing at him before hurrying off to class. I think she's always liked him. Maybe that's why she was mean to Layla and unpegged that tent. Anyway, Mum said it's good to try and forgive, and I have, definitely.

People do things for reasons – just like Ben.

He's gone now, and the bell has rung. Mr Saunders, our science teacher, smiles as he walks past Layla and me. "Are you two going to stand there all day dreaming?" he asks.

We laugh and follow him to the classroom, ready to start a new day.

Chapter thirty
Four months later

Ben

I'm back down south now, near Brighton. That bit was true. Not the boarding school part; I was never a boarder — though, weirdly, that's what I'm going to be now. It's the start of my new life after a long, hot summer. My ankle and arm are finally free of plaster casts, and the scar on my face is still there, but fading slowly.

I don't mind it. It's my souvenir from those few short weeks when so much happened. Kyle, Danny, Harris and Jude — I wonder if they'll remember me. And Zoe and Layla. . . I hadn't been used to girls liking me, that was the problem. At my old school, there weren't any. But even if there had been, they'd never have looked at me. The kids at that school were clever beyond belief. *Future leaders of this country*, Dad used to tell us. Can you imagine, being one of the dumbest kids in your school where your own dad is the deputy head? No wonder the other boys hated me.

When I came up with the plan to have a mini festival in the school grounds, I didn't think it'd make me popular. I just wanted to make music and show everyone what a great time we could have. And I was sick to death of all the rules and regulations.

New Year's Eve, it was. Anyone I knew who played an instrument, I persuaded them to come along. Actually, they didn't need much persuading. Just like moths, everyone surged towards the massive bonfire we built – it was the best night ever. Well, maybe the fire wasn't such a good idea. I'd got carried away and hadn't realized it would completely ruin the school football pitch. And then, of course, there were police and fire engines and not even Dad could stop me from being suspended from school...

An *event*, that's what I'd wanted. Something amazing, that everyone would talk about and remember for ever. I wanted to make things happen. I guess I always have. Sending me to Aunt Mary's was supposed to be a punishment, but it wasn't really. I loved it there.

Still, at least my parents have agreed that I can make the choice this time.

So here I am, in Dad's big black BMW pulling up in the school car park. It's not like Mossbridge, which was a modern building. Raven's Gate Arts Academy is all red brick and vast grounds with woodland and even a lake. Mum, Dad and I climb out of the car. The atmosphere between us is kind of awkward but immediately, it feels right being here.

Already, a couple of girls and a boy have glanced over and said hi. From an open window I can hear someone playing piano, and a boy of around my age has strolled past, carrying a guitar. Groups of students are sprawled on the grass. It's a warm, sunny September morning, and the new term starts today. Somehow, I don't think I'll have to invent a new persona to be here.

"Let's go in then," Mum says, smiling hesitantly. She's nervous around me, perhaps because I'm so different to my genius big brothers, and she doesn't know how to handle that.

"OK," I say, picking up my guitar. Dad goes to take my wheeled suitcase, but I grip its handle firmly.

"I can manage, Dad," I say with a smile.

His face relaxes as the three of us head towards the school entrance.

We meet Miss Boyle at the office. We've been here already and she's shown me around, and seemed impressed that I've had a home tutor these past few weeks. How to wreck someone's summer, huh? Anyway, she's all smiles and laughter as she takes me up to my room.

"I wish he'd had his hair cut," I hear Dad muttering to Mum behind us.

"You'll be sharing with Anthony and James," Miss Boyle says as I set my bag on the floor of the bright, sunny room. "Now," she adds, turning to my parents, "I'd like to introduce Benedict to some of the other students. . ."

Time to go, is what she means.

"Well, we'd better be off," Dad says quickly.

"Yes, of course," Mum says, giving me an anxious glance. We all head back down the grand, curving staircase out into the grounds. I hug Mum, then Dad, and there's something different about it. It's warmer, more real. But I'm still relieved when they turn to give a final wave, climb into the car and drive away.

There's a burst of laughter from a group of girls. Two in particular catch my eye – a tall, sporty-looking blonde one, a bit like Zoe, in a vest top and tracksuit bottoms, and a smaller girl with a tumble of dark curls.

Miss Boyle smiles. "I've asked a couple of girls to show you round, if that's OK."

"Yes, great."

She shields her eyes against the sun and beckons them over. "Chloe? Bryony? Would you come over here, please?" They turn and look, first at her, then at me. "Remember I talked to you about showing our new arrival around?" Miss Boyle says.

They head towards me, perhaps seeing my scar, perhaps not. I don't care. It's just a part of me now. "Hi," the blonde one says, blushing slightly.

I push back my hair, reminding myself that I don't have to pretend to be something I'm not. This is me now, the *real* me, no more lies. "Hi," I say with my brightest smile, "I'm Ben."